orca sports

LUCKY BREAK

BROOKE CARTER

ORCA BOOK PUBLISHERS

Library and Archives Canada Cataloguing in Publication

Carter, Brooke 1977–, author
Lucky Break / Brooke Carter.
(Orca sports)

Issued in print and electronic formats.
ISBN 978-1-4598-1641-1 (softcover).—ISBN 978-1-4598-1642-8 (PDF).—
ISBN 978-1-4598-1643-5 (EPUB)

I. Title. II. Series: Orca sports
PS8605.A77776L83 2018   jc813'.6   c2017-907915-8
                               c2017-907916-6

First published in the United States, 2018
Library of Congress Control Number: 2018933701

Summary: In this high-interest sports novel for young readers, Lucy
"Lucky" Graves breaks her leg in a rugby game and jeopardizes her future.
A free teacher guide for this title is available at orcabook.com.

MIX
Paper from
responsible sources
FSC® C016245

*Orca Book Publishers is dedicated to preserving the environment and
has printed this book on Forest Stewardship Council® certified paper.*

Orca Book Publishers gratefully acknowledges the support for
its publishing programs provided by the following agencies:
the Government of Canada through the Canada Book Fund and
the Canada Council for the Arts, and the Province of British Columbia
through the BC Arts Council and the Book Publishing Tax Credit.

Edited by Tanya Trafford
Cover photography by UVic Vikes/APShutter.com
Author photo by Laura Housden

ORCA BOOK PUBLISHERS
orcabook.com

Printed and bound in Canada.

21 20 19 18 • 4 3 2 1

*For my daughters, my two
lucky charms.*

Chapter One
Who Am I?

My name is Lucy Graves and I am a rugby player. I'm supposed to be writing the essay portion of my scholarship application, and it has to be so dazzling that I score all the full-ride money I need to attend college. How's it going? Not so dazzling. It's nearing the end of third period, I'm in the cave-like school library holed up at one of the quiet back study tables, and I'm stuck. The essay prompt is an open-ended question that I just can't answer. On the scholarship form in bold, cartoony letters is the question:

WHO AM I?

I'll let that sink in for a moment.

What straight-up psycho wrote this question? How many seventeen-year-olds can answer it? Not me. After all, I'm not just one thing all the time. If there's anything true about me, it's that I'm existing in a constant state of chaos. Hello, I'm in high school.

For example. I'm a student athlete trying to maintain my straight-A average while I train nonstop to be the best rugby player this school has ever seen. I'm also a carboholic (I've got this super important championship-qualifying game after school—no biggie) and sometimes I need mac and cheese like my life depends on it. My life might actually depend on winning this game, so I ate a container that I brought from home in the few minutes I had between classes.My jampacked schedule doesn't allow for a proper lunch break, so I eat when I can. This afternoon, when my well-meaning guidance counselor, Ms. Bean, handed me the form with her pointy fake nails, she encouraged me to fill it out and include as many personal details as possible. Fine, here goes.

VERY IMPORTANT
FACTS ABOUT ME

1. I am the daughter of a single mother (who is completely awesome, by the way).
2. I am biracial (my mom is pasty white Irish, and my dad was a black man from Trinidad, thank you very much).
3. I have a strong academic record (I take all advanced-placement courses).
4. I am Blue Mountain High's top athlete (and not just top female athlete, ahem).
5. In case you didn't catch the past tense in item #2, I have a dead dad (oh yeah, it's completely tragic).
6. I like to make lists (it calms me down).

Okay, the fifth and sixth points might be overkill. The scholarship people don't really need to know my sad story, do they? They definitely don't need to know about my borderline OCD. Did I say "borderline"? I meant crippling. Ha!

Okay, focus. *My name is Lucy Graves and I am a rugby player.* Who am I? Well, right now I'm an emotional wreck because if I don't get my team to the finals, and if I don't win, then I won't secure my status as the best fly-half Blue Mountain High has ever seen, and I won't get an athletic scholarship, and I won't go to college to play rugby, and I won't get the education that my mom can't afford, and I won't see the world, and I won't get a good job, and I won't ever become anything important, and I might as well curl up and die right now because, as the great Mariah Carey would say, my future is bleak, bleak, bleak.

My name is Lucy Graves and I am a rugby player. God, why can't I get past this thought? *Stop thinking about it, Lucy.* I shift my focus to watching video replays on my phone of last season's games against our main rivals, the Riverside Grizzlies. They're the ones we're playing today, and I am not looking forward to it.

As I listen to the sound of rugby through my earbuds, it transports me back to the last game we played against the Grizzlies.

Mud squelching, players yelling to each other, whistles blowing. The ball hurtles toward me as I run through the pouring rain. I reach for it with fingers numbed by cold and feel its textured surface make contact. There's no time to hesitate. I plant my posts deep in the slippery field to secure my footing in the mud before hugging the ball close and taking off down the pitch. Blood whooshes in my ears. My body burns hot. Push past the pain in your knees, Lucy. Push past the pain in your lungs. The constant pain in your neck.

The opposing team thunders toward me as I weave through their huge defensive players. Their props and locks aim to take me down hard, throwing their bodies at me with abandon as I run past. My teammates shout to one another along the length of the field, waiting to catch the ball if I toss it back to them. They keep just behind me so we don't drive the play offside. I'm almost there.

"Hard!" Coach Stevens yells from the sideline. I've got to pour it on now. Footfalls pound behind me, gaining on me. The other team is close, but I'm closer. With a final surge I cross the try line. I stumble and feel the rough embrace of my pursuer on the back of my jersey. We fall in a tumble of knees and elbows and cleats, but it's too late for the other team. I've scored the winning points of the game with only seconds to spare. I'd jump up and celebrate with my screaming teammates, but I'm too gassed out to move. I lie on the soaking-wet grass, feeling alive, sucking air, covered in mud and grime and sweat. I taste blood on my lower lip. I must have bitten it, but it doesn't matter. The pain is worth it. It's always worth it.

Watching the video, I can see just how close I had been to being taken down. Half a second slower and I would have been toast. I could have passed the ball during my charge several times, but I was too focused on myself. When I'm in the zone I just can't help it. I had to run to the try line. I had to win.

TOP FIVE THINGS
I LOVE ABOUT RUGBY

1. The contact (I love to get tackled, and I love how rough it is).
2. Running (nothing makes me feel more alive).
3. Scoring (what can I say? I live for the glory).
4. Outsmarting the other team (so satisfying).
5. The temporary calm I feel after a match (the only time I feel calm).

The Blue Mountain Eagles, the girls rugby team at my high school, is one of the best in the district, but the Riverside Grizzlies have us beat in the size department by a wide margin. The last time we played them was not pretty. We won (barely), and we were hurting for weeks.

As I absentmindedly palm the trusty and tattered rugby ball I carry with me everywhere, I search the video footage for some clue, some weakness we can exploit. It's up to me as team captain to call the plays on the field, and I don't know if I can find a way to beat them. Not without all of us getting maimed anyway.

My name is Lucy Graves and I am a rugby player. I can feel my stomach starting to burn and I wonder how much Pepto-Bismol I'll have to chug before going out on the field so I don't barf up stomach acid. Who am I? I'm seventeen and I'm pretty sure I have an ulcer. My mostly uneaten snack sits on the library table—it's the same disgusting-slash-amazing Graves family secret recipe potato-salad sandwich my mom makes me on game days because she knows how I like to keep everything the same. And also, CARBS. But today the first bite of the sandwich got stuck going down, and ever since then I've felt like I have a rock lodged in my throat. It's getting

is Lucy Graves and I am a rugby player. I seriously cannot stop this thought! It's stuck on some kind of loop.

"It's fine," says Mr. Princely Redhead. "I quite like talking to myself as well. Sometimes I sit here in the library and have a little chat with myself about fractions or prime numbers."

"Uh..." I'm not winning any awards for being clever today. "You what?"

He laughs, and when he does his nose crinkles up and his freckles scrunch together, the pattern of spots looking sort of like the number three. It's so cute that I grin in spite of myself. And then quickly stop. I don't want him to see. Too late. He's grinning back.

"Andy," he says. "Andrew, really, but Andy is what I'm called. Andy Williams." Now it's his turn to sound awkward. "We use the same AP Math lab, yeah?"

He's right. I've definitely noticed him before, but I've been so busy with training and the rugby season that I haven't spent much time scoping out the landscape of the school, so to speak. I'm definitely scoping now though.

"Yeah," I manage. "Math." It's one of my better subjects because I find the reliability of numbers to be soothing. But right now I'm not coming across as much of a brainiac.

The bell rings and I jump a little. I've been totally staring at him.

He smiles, gathers his books and approaches my table. "I'm excited to score with you later."

Hold up. "What did you just say to me?" I stand up.

He's tall, but so am I, and I've been known to tackle opponents well over two hundred pounds. Freckles or no freckles, Mr. Princely Redhead better watch himself.

"I-I," he stammers, his face flushing an adorable shade of crimson to match his hair. "I meant I'm scoring the game. Later. I'm keeping score. Coach Stevens asked me to do it because Ben Whitley is sick. So I'm doing the scoreboard thing. I'm keeping track of the, uh, touchdowns."

"Touchdowns?"

"Y-yeah. Please don't hit me."

"Why would I do that?"

"Because," he says, pointing to my hands, "you're making fists."

I look down. My knuckles are white. "No! I wasn't going to hit you. I just do that when I'm nervous." I unclench my hands and feel the blood rush back to my fingertips. Maybe he was closer to getting knocked out than either of us thought.

He smiles, and his shoulders relax. He's out of danger. "I'm sure you'll be great. You're the best in the school, aren't you?"

"No. I'm the best in the district, probably the province."

"Well, I'm happy to see you've got a healthy dose of self-esteem."

"No, I just really am that good. I mean, I can't cook, I can't sew, I hate writing essays, I don't dance, I'm a terrible singer. But rugby...rugby is my thing."

"Right. Lucy Graves, rugby player. Got it. Won't forget."

"Anyway," I add, "guys boast about their athletic prowess, so why can't I?"

"I agree completely. Like, I could not agree more. Prowess. Good stuff." He gives me a thumbs-up.

"Good." I laugh. "By the way," I add as I pick up my ball and turn to leave, "it's not called a touchdown. It's called a *try*, and it's worth five points. Unless, of course, it's converted, in which case it's worth seven. And you can expect a lot of those. I'm the kicker."

"So I've heard. I guess I better brush up on my rugby rules."

"Aren't you British? Isn't it a major sin to be a Brit and not know the rules of rugby?"

"Well, I'm not British. I was born in New Zealand. And my family isn't really 'sporty.' Both of my parents are accountants. I probably will be too. Boring, I know." He chuckles and looks down at his feet.

"New Zealand? The land of my favorite rugby team?"

He stares at me.

"The All Blacks?" I say, shaking my head. "How can you be from the same country as the best rugby players in the world and not be a fan?"

FAST FACTS ABOUT THE ALL BLACKS

1. The New Zealand men's rugby team.
2. All Blacks is a nickname, thought to come from the color of the team uniform or a typo in an article, but really it's just a super cool name.
3. Have won more games than any other team in history.
4. Have been playing since 1884.
5. I desperately want to go to New Zealand to see them play on their home turf.

"Well, perhaps I can be converted," Andy says. "Maybe watching you today will inspire me." He smiles and dips his head again, and a little piece of red hair flops forward across his forehead.

Am I crazy or is this adorable redheaded guy flirting with me? Don't get me wrong—I think I can draw my fair share of attention from boys. I'm fit and interesting-looking. I have my dad's dark skin and my mom's fine features. It's just that all I have room for in my life is rugby and schoolwork. I wish I was better at balancing things. I'm always in a state of near-panic, and feel as if any minute I'm going to implode.

"Something I said?" Andy asks. He's regarding me with a kind, concerned look.

"Huh?" I realize I've been staring sadly into the middle distance like some sort of pathetic teen-movie heroine.

"I'm just nervous about this game," I say. "It's super important, and I need all the luck I can get. My teammates call me Lucky because I'm half Irish and I was born on St. Patrick's Day. Also, I always win the coin tosses at the start of games. I find money on the street all the time. I win at Bingo during fundraising nights, and I have a knack for finding four-leaf clovers.

Seven so far. But that doesn't mean I'm actually all that lucky."

"How are you not lucky?" he asks. "It sounds like you've got a rabbit's foot..." He trails off and swallows hard.

I laugh. "A rabbit's foot stuck up my butt? Yeah, I've heard that one."

"Sorry," he says, laughing too. "But you seem..."

"What?"

"I don't know," he says. "Golden, I guess. Like the kind of person everything works out for. The opposite of me," he adds, smiling. "I've been known to break mirrors, walk under ladders, encounter too many black cats. That sort of thing."

"I'm not golden," I say. "Far from it."

"Why?" he asks. Something in his eyes tells me that he really does want to know.

"Because," I say after a moment, "even though I'm the captain of a championship girls' rugby team—the only team that ever wins anything for Blue Mountain High, by the way—it seems like people only see me as that jock chick with the wild hair who's always eating and never goes to parties and isn't girly enough. The opposite of golden. Dull."

He's staring at me. Why do I babble like this around cute boys? *Shut up, Lucy.*

He fills the awkward silence that follows. "Well," he says, "I like your ratty thingamabob." He points to the rugby ball in my hands.

I laugh. "Thingamabob?"

"Err, I gather it's some sort of sporting device, but judging by all the tape holding it together, I imagine it hasn't actually been used for legit sports stuff for a long time." He grins at me. Yep, definitely flirting.

I take in his tidy but not-at-all-stuffy appearance. Clean fingernails, preppy clothes—although I do notice he's wearing ratty Converse sneakers.

"It's a talisman of sorts." I toss the ball up and catch it. "My lucky ball."

I glance at the big clock on the back library wall. It's getting late.

"Sorry, I've got to go." I hurry toward the exit.

"Okay," he says, his voice cheerful. "I'll see you out on the, er, field?"

"The pitch," I call over my shoulder. "It's called a pitch."

I glance back as I push through the heavy library doors. Yep, he's definitely checking me out. *Focus, Lucy, focus.*

My name is Lucy Graves and I am a rugby player. Yes, and this rugby player better get herself to the locker room to prep. I've got a game to win.

Chapter Three
The Cap Of Doom

My name is Lucy Graves and I am overwhelmed. What else is new? I have organized my class schedule so that fourth period is my free block. This way I can prep in the afternoons before practices and games. Because I don't get an official lunch break, it means that from the time I get up in the morning until after I'm done with practices and games and training (which is every day in some form) and homework, I go, go, go. I don't get a lot of sleep because my mind races all night with everything that I have to do the next day.

I'm one of those people who is pathologically early to everything. To me, there's nothing worse than showing up without a moment to spare—not to a movie, a class, a practice or a game. I've always envied my teammates who can just breeze through the locker room, toss on their gear and run out onto the pitch. It's like everyone else was born ready, and I've got to work for every single moment.

I'm already feeling the pressure rise in my chest as I hurry through the halls. That little chat with Andy has made me later than usual, put a little wrench in my schedule. I don't adapt to so-called wrenches. In fact, it seems like this school year has been harder than the last. Each new responsibility piles on top to create a mountain of discomfort. I'm going to graduate soon and I don't know what will happen next.

As I pass other students I smile and nod or give a little wave to the ones I'm friendly with. I'm not unpopular, but most of my relationships revolve around school projects or my team.

I'm almost at the locker-room doors when Mr. McCabe, my math teacher, steps out into the hall in front of me. He's been after me for weeks to sign up for Mathletes, and he will not leave me alone.

"Graves," he says, drawing the name out like he's addressing a Bond villain. It's extra funny because he's not exactly a snappy dresser. Today he's wearing green pants with a purple plaid shirt and a sweater vest. He looks like a nerdy Joker. I wonder what Mrs. McCabe thinks when he leaves the house every morning.

"McCabe," I counter, equally dramatic.

We stand looking at each other for a long moment, and he smiles a little and motions to his classroom.

"If you'll indulge me a moment," he says.

"Actually—" I begin, but he cuts me off.

"You can spare a moment, Graves."

I can't be rude to Mr. McCabe. He's a teacher, and my mom would kill me if she ever heard about me being less than polite to any of my teachers.

I scoot into the empty classroom and hop up onto one of the desks. Mr. McCabe's walls are covered with those wooden signs you can buy at craft fairs, all of them with super hokey sayings painted or engraved on them. There must be at least fifty signs.

McCABE'S CHEESY SIGN COLLECTION

40 isn't old if you're a tree.
Live, laugh, love.
Believe in yourself.
Be a rainbow in someone else's cloud.
The best things in life aren't things.
Stressed spelled backward is desserts.
Keep calm and do the math.
Slow down, happiness is trying to catch you.

I like the last one because it's ironic. Happiness, for me, means outrunning everyone else.

"You know, Mr. McCabe, your love of cheesy signage is truly baffling."

"That so?"

"I mean, you're this smart, rational mathematician..."

"Thanks," he says.

"...and yet you decorate your room like an old lady," I add. "Seriously, my grandma would love this junk."

He shrugs.

I spot a new one above his desk. It says *2+2=5*. I point to it. "A *1984* reference? Orwell? Nice."

He nods. "Always good to remind today's youth of the mistakes of the past. History repeating itself and all of that."

"But *1984* is fiction."

"Is it, Graves?"

"Funny. I'm still not joining Mathletes."

"Dang it." He sits down on the desk across from me, picks up a jelly sandwich and begins chewing in defeat. He offers me half.

I shake my head.

"When are you going to come around, Graves? We need you. *Math* needs you. You can't let the Math down."

"I can't. Rugby takes too much time. And I've got to apply for scholarships." I motion to the stack of papers tucked under my arm. Even though the Mathletes team (probably the only other extracurricular activity Blue Mountain is known for) does look fun, I just don't have the time. "If you can figure out a way to add several hours to each day, then I'll do it."

"You know," says Mr. McCabe, "those athletic scholarships are tough to qualify for. Rugby, especially women's rugby, isn't the kind of sport that gets a ton of funding. Not around here. And I know more than a few qualified athletes in the district are competing for the same dollars."

"Are you trying to discourage me? I thought you wanted me to succeed."

"I just want you to keep your options open. There are more scholarships available for academics, especially for someone as gifted as you. Believe me, Lucy, there's money in Math. It can take you places rugby can't."

"Like teaching at Blue Mountain High?" My voice comes out sounding so snotty, like one of the awful girls from my math tutorial. *Who am I?*

He winces. "Ouch, Graves. Direct hit."

"I'm sorry." I really am. Sometimes I just blurt things out that I don't even mean. "I've got to work on keeping my mouth shut."

"No, you're right." He puts his half-eaten sandwich back on the desk. "But you can't compare yourself to me. I wasn't focused at your age, and I made different choices. I don't regret anything. But we're talking about you right now. You have real potential. Your brain is your asset, Lucy, not just how fast and strong you are out on the pitch."

"Speaking of which," I say, "I've got to get ready for the game."

Mr. McCabe nods. "Okay, Lucy. I will admit defeat. For now."

"Thanks, Mr. McCabe. See you out there?"

"Always. Break a leg, kid."

I hurry out, feeling like my skin isn't fitting right. I squeeze my rugby ball closer and almost drop my papers in the hall. My hands are sweaty.

"It's just the anxiety. I need to get out onto the pitch," I whisper to myself and then look around to see if anyone is watching me. The halls are blessedly empty.

The pitch is the only place where I can slow things down. Rugby is a fast-paced sport, but when I play, it's like I can see time and space open up on the field. Rugby is about making space, moving into that space and using it to get where you want to go.

Life is seriously getting harder and harder to manage. When I feel like this I go back to my lists.

FUN RUGBY TERMS

1. Dummy pass: A trick pass you use to draw defenders to the wrong player. It makes space for the true ball carrier.
2. Garryowen: A short, high kick that goes right on top of or just behind the defending team. It's named after a rugby club in Ireland that famously used this tactic.
3. Goose step: When you're running and you slow down and then jump up before taking off in a different direction. It confuses your opponent.
4. Hospital pass: When you pass the ball, but the receiver is definitely going to be tackled immediately.
5. Sin bin: Where you have to go and sit for ten minutes when you get a yellow card.

I push open the locker-room doors, and the familiar sour smell hits me full force. It's disgusting and comforting. The linoleum-lined room is empty save for its ancient wood benches and banks of lockers. I will have it all to myself for a few minutes. I take a deep breath and, as is part of my ritual, spin around and step backward into the room.

Part of being lucky, of being prepared, is also about being superstitious. At least, it is for me. Every single time I enter this locker room, I do so backward. And I always go directly to my locker, number ten, my lucky number, and lock and relock my combination lock ten times. It's time-consuming, but it calms me down. That calming feeling is also why I tie and retie my rugby boots— my cleats—ten times.

If the game is on a Tuesday, like it is today, I always wear my jersey inside out until right before the game starts. I also have a notebook that I keep my lists, charts and breakdowns of all my stats in.

I'm not the only one like this. A lot of my teammates have quirky habits too. Some of them won't shave their legs, or they always put a certain boot on first, or they always wear a particular tank top. The pro players also have some pretty crazy rituals and habits. For example, the Wales national rugby team engages in habitual vomiting. Yep, before games they barf on purpose. The whole team pukes as a group. I guess they don't want a lot of heavy food in their bellies before they play, but that's one ritual I won't partake in. Why not just skip eating the "rarebit" and "cockles" and all the other weird Welsh foods in the first place?

The locker-room door slams open and our team's newest member, Jenny, our number seven openside flanker, hurtles into the room. Her face is red and it isn't from exercise. She's been crying.

"What's up?" I ask.

"Lucy, I don't know if I can do this," she says, looking like she's about to vomit.

"You're not going to spew, are you?" I ask. "This isn't the Welsh team, honey, so don't puke in here."

"No, I'm just mega nervous." She looks down at her feet.

Even though she's inexperienced, during tryouts Jenny ran the length of the pitch two full seconds faster than anyone else. We need her.

"Sit, girl." I motion to the bench across from me.

She sits and starts chewing on her thumbnail.

"What's your job?" I ask.

"Um, I'm the outside flanker. I win balls at the ruck and maul. And I collect short passes."

"Good," I say. "We are all relying on you to do your job. Just focus on that and you'll be fine. You're about to earn your first cap!"

She brightens a little at this. "Yeah, I just wish the other team wasn't so huge."

Oh, now I get it. She's afraid of getting hurt in her first official game. She's taking over from Shelly Sharma, since Shelly tore all the ligaments in her right knee.

"Yes," I agree. "They're big. But we're faster. And it's hard to tackle what you can't catch."

She grins. "Yeah."

"So don't get caught," I add.

"I can't wait until I have a thousand caps like you," she says.

I laugh. "One hundred and seventy-four, including today's game."

"Whoa. One hundred and seventy-four," she echoes me.

One hundred and seventy-four. I realize the numbers add up to 12. Now I'm the one who feels like puking. "Everything bad in my life can be traced back to 12," I mutter.

Jenny looks confused. "Lucy, are you okay?"

I'm talking to myself again. "I'm fine. Just overthinking." *Stop it, Lucy. Don't think about it.*

I lean down and retie my rugby boots. They don't look right. I pull the laces and retie them. I look to the row of light switches on the wall that control the overhead fluorescents and imagine myself flicking them all off and on. The skin on my neck feels like it's getting tighter, like someone's inflating a blood-pressure cuff around my throat.

I reach back and touch the raised seven-centimeter scar at my nape. *I was 12 years old when I got this.* I stretch my neck, trying to shake the stiffness threatening to take over. *No, not right now. Not today. Not again.*

The locker-room door swings open, and the rest of the girls stream in. I'm grateful for the distraction and turn away from Jenny to focus on my breathing. The room is filled with the sound of girls chattering, equipment clattering, tape pulling from rolls and personal playlists blasting out from portable speakers.

I count the seconds until game time, and as the numbers climb in my mind I feel the pressure in my neck subside. I need to make sure all the players are here, so I get up and walk the room, making a mental note of each girl.

Everyone is here except for number eight, Miss Emily Jones. Just as my annoyance at her absence is peaking, she comes rushing into the room. As usual, she's here at the last moment with barely enough time to get changed. She is carrying a bundle of wrinkled gear, plus keys, cell phone, lip gloss, books, cleats and her open backpack. All of it is threatening to spill onto the sticky locker-room floor.

Emily is a problem, a roadblock to my ultimate goal: to get out of this town. She's also my closest friend. Emily is nice, smart, fun to be around and a fantastic rugby player. As the "eighth-man" (number 8), she's an important play caller, and we have a kind of sixth sense on the field. She always seems to know where to pass before I even get there. She's also the assistant captain of the team. We're both going to need the dough for college, and there's limited funding for female sport scholarships, but Emily's financial situation is better than mine. She has options. Her dad is the town's go-to orthodontist, and her mom runs a decorating business complete with one of those minivans that has the company logo shrink-wrapped all over it. I know Emily's life isn't perfect, and that being gorgeous and well-off doesn't make things any easier, but I do wonder if she stays awake all night worrying like I do. Does she feel trapped like I do? Does she second-guess every decision like I do? Does she wish she could go back in time like I do? Sometimes just looking at her makes my chest hurt.

My envy for Emily is an ugly secret, and I try hard not to let it show. It's not something I've told anyone—not even my mom. When our eyes meet I smile and nod, and she hustles over to me.

"Oh my god, Lucky," she says. "You would not believe the cluster at the cafeteria." She rolls her eyes.

This is a familiar tale. There's always some long lineup or situation somewhere that keeps Emily from being on time.

"All I wanted in the entire universe was an egg roll, and do you think I could get one? No! I waited almost twenty minutes and by the time I got to the front of the line all they had left were soggy crumbs. God, Lucky. It was so tragic."

"That sounds awful," I deadpan, but I secretly sympathize. We both love food, and that's one of the greatest things about our chosen sport. It's not good to be skinny as a rugby player. You need muscle for protection.

Emily throws on her gear, flipping her long blond hair out from her collar. She's got straight, white teeth, clear skin and the face of a teen model. She's tall and lean with six-pack abs and calves of steel. She's fast. She's smart. And she's key to us winning this game.

"Emily," I say. "Are you ready?"

"Are you kidding, Lucky?" She tosses an old hair tie at me. "I was born ready."

"Let's get everyone else ready."

Together we round up the girls, making sure they all have their mouthguards and that the locks have their scrum caps, and we usher them toward the outer locker-room doors that open onto the field at the back of the school.

Just before Emily pushes open the doors, she pauses, turns and asks the team the same question she always does.

"WHO ARE WE?" she yells in her most cheerful, motivating voice. The irony of this question is not lost on me.

"EAGLES!" the team shouts back.

"WHAT DO WE LOVE?" I yell. My voice sounds less powerful than it usually does.

"RUGBY!" the team yells.

"WHAT ARE WE GOING TO DO?" Emily and I yell together.

"WIN!" we all yell together.

Emily pushes down on the metal door bar, and the doors fling open, flooding the locker room with daylight. She stands aside for me.

I take a deep breath. I am always the first one out. From this point on, this team is my responsibility. I have to keep them safe. I have to call good plays. I have to run hard and score. I have to win.

Chapter Four
Perfect 10

My name is Lucy Graves and I am a fly-half. Following my lead, the team runs out onto the school grounds, across the gravel track and onto the field. I can see Coach Stevens setting up gear. The referees are busy checking over the field markings.

As we jog over, I look down the field. I don't see the other team. Their bus must not have arrived, or else they're still getting ready in one of the gym bathrooms we designated for visiting teams. Part of me hopes they won't show up and that they'll forfeit. Forget that. We're going to play them, and we're going to beat them.

I jog up to Coach Stevens as the rest of the team starts to run laps around the field. They'll do four slow laps—enough to get warm and limber but not enough to tire out. I would normally join them, but I need to talk to Coach.

"Hey, Coach." I help her unload the game balls and other supplies from the big duffel bag she carries.

"Lucky." She smiles and brushes her frizzy sandy-colored bangs from her eyes.

Her hair and her tanned skin are almost the same color, and I've always liked how she looks as if she just stepped in from a windstorm.

"You ready for today?" she asks.

"Yeah. A bit nervous, but you know how it is."

She does know. Coach Stevens played college rugby until an injury sidelined her professional career. She still has the rugby-player look—tall, broad-shouldered, muscular and super fit.

"This match will be hard work," she says. Coach always tells it like it is. "But I think we can pull it off. I'm going to need you and Emily to get a lot of short passes going, lots of fast footwork and lots of kicks. We need to make space out there. Those Grizzlies are coming in heavy."

She nods behind her. Right on cue, the Grizzlies come running out onto the field in formation. They're even bigger than they were before—or at least they seem like it. I recognize their captain right away because of the evil number emblazoned across her jersey. Number 12. She is the Grizzlies' powerful inside center. Her position is all action, and she dishes out tackles like she's taking a leisurely walk. Her name is Samantha something, and I took several hits from her the last time we faced off. *Why does she have to be number 12?*

"You okay?" Coach asks.

I nod, but she doesn't look convinced.

"Lucy," she says. "This is just one game."

"I know. But it's one of the most important—"

A voice from behind me interrupts. "Hey, Lucy Graves, rugby player."

I see Coach's eyebrows go up as she looks past me to the speaker.

I know who it is even before I turn around. Andy Williams, Expert-level Distractor.

"Um," I start, at a loss for words.

Coach cuts in. "Oh, Andy, you can get set up on the other side of the field. Lucy will help you with that." She motions to the scoreboard number signs at Andy's feet. She smiles at me and winks.

"Yeah, sure," I say as I gather up the heavy laminated squares. Blue Mountain doesn't have the budget for an electronic scoreboard on the secondary field we play on. There is one on the main field where the boys' football team plays, even though they haven't won a championship in years.

"Thanks," Andy says as he follows me across the grass.

As we walk, my team trots past, and several of them stare at us and mouth silently, *Oh my god* and *Cuuuute* and

Girl while I hope he doesn't notice. But of course he does.

I look at Andy, and I get a little thrill when he looks at me and mouths the word *Wow.*

I don't know if it's being out on the field, or the energy I get before a game, or the fact that I feel like myself in my uniform, but I feel way less nervous around him now.

"Thanks for doing this," I say, dropping the boards on the sideline. "It's hard to get resources for our games."

"The players on the other team don't look like they're fooling around," he says.

I follow his gaze to the far end of the field. The Grizzlies are doing push-ups and tackling drills.

"Yeah," I reply. "But we're not fooling around either. We're prepared. We did the work."

Andy motions to my jersey. "Number 10, hey? That's fitting."

"Fitting? Why?"

"Well, because you're so...hot." I swear he doesn't blush even a tiny bit.

My face, on the other hand, feels like it's on fire. *Wow*, I mouth silently, because I literally can't think of anything else.

"Is that your lucky number?" he asks, unfazed.

"No, I'm number 10 because I'm the fly-half."

He stares at me.

"It's my position," I explain.

"Wait, is that how it works?" he asks, surprised.

I laugh. He is adorably ignorant about rugby. He's so cute that I don't care.

I indulge him. "Number 10 is always the fly-half on a rugby team. That's me. To play fly-half you've got to be the calmest and least emotional member of the team."

"Why is that?" he asks.

"Because we do a lot of the kicking, the conversions, penalties and stuff like that. You need to be calm to kick. You need accurate feet, you have to be great at passing, and you still have to be able to tackle—all while maintaining top speeds. It's one of the most important positions.

I'm the brains, basically, and my choices dictate the way our team will play."

"Hmm," he says, frowning a little. "That's not giving your team a lot of credit."

I'm a bit confused by his response. *Am I being arrogant?*

"Don't get me wrong," I explain quickly. "Every position is important. But some positions are vital to the way a match turns out. I'm a key decision-maker. I've got to be totally confident if I'm going to lead us to a win. My team depends on me."

"Sounds like a lot of pressure," he says, and something about the sad way he says it makes me think he can relate.

"Yeah," I say quietly. "It is."

"Lucky!" Emily calls out to me, motioning for me to come.

Coach has the team organized in formation and is going over the strategy.

"It's not that complicated. Just don't get murdered," I mutter under my breath.

"Huh?" Andy cocks his head at me.

"Never mind. Catch you later." I smile at Andy and jog off to join my team.

He stares after me with a full smile on his face. God, he's cute.

I pick up the pace a bit and add some high knees as I approach my team. I missed laps, so I've got to catch up. As I break into jumping jacks, I see Emily eyeing me and nodding toward Andy as if to say, *What's the deal?* I shrug and continue my jumping jacks.

"Jenny, take the team through the stretches," Coach says. Jenny is nervously pacing next to me.

Happy for the distraction, she leads us through our safety stretches. We never skip this part. We carefully rotate all our joints through their range of motion and make sure everything is warm and loose.

"Lucky," says Emily. "Your mom is here."

Mom? I spin around and see her standing on the sideline. What is she doing here? I hope nothing bad has happened. She should be at work.

I jog over to Coach. "Is it okay if I go check in with my mom really quick?"

She nods, and I run over.

"Hey," I say, running up to Mom. "What's the matter? I thought you had to work tonight?"

I notice she is wearing an All Blacks jersey with the number 10 on it. My number. Dad's old number from when he used to play in college.

Mom smiles. "This game's an important one, right? Anyway, I wanted to see you play."

My mother is one of those people who is so beautiful that people stare wherever she goes. I'm lucky that I sort of look like her. Well, we have the same eye shape, though hers are blue. She's the definition of all-American good looks. Seriously, someone should pay her to model for those inserts that come in photo frames. I am definitely not that.

People always assume I'm adopted when they meet Mom, especially because my dad isn't around. I was 12 years old when he died.

"Thanks for coming," I say. "Can you stay for the whole game?"

She shakes her head. "No, kiddo, sorry. I'm going to have get back to the office to get caught up. Hope that's okay. Were you planning on doing anything after the game?"

"Me? No. Just homework. It's cool." I know Mom needs to work. She's made a decent career for herself by doing the books of several local businesses. I get my love of math and order from her.

"Okay, get out there and kick some Grizzly butt for me, will you?"

"I'll bring you back a bearskin rug." I run off to take my place on the field.

Chapter Five
Drop-Kicked

My name is Lucy Graves and I'm the kicker. Every rugby match starts with a kickoff. The coaches of each team have settled on a game ball, and the referee and two touch judges have the clock set and their whistles ready. Andy has the score-board set up.

The spectators hoot and holler their support. As I jog out to midfield I see that Mr. McCabe has taken a seat in the stands next to my mom. Probably trying to get her help recruiting me for Mathletes.

My cleats dig down into the dirt as I run. My heart thrums in my chest. I don't even look at the other team. They don't exist. I keep my eyes on my teammates. Each girl is in position and watching me in return. I raise my fist, and they raise theirs back. We've got this.

I stop at center field, where the Grizzlies' captain is already pacing in a slow circle and stretching out her hamstrings. Evil Number 12. She stands a full head taller than me.

"I'm not intimidated. I'm in the zone," I whisper to myself.

"What did you say?" Evil Number 12 advances, getting right up in my face. "You quit already?"

"Never." I smirk at her.

"Wait until we're done with you," she says.

"Ladies, save it." The referee approaches. He holds up a quarter. It's time to flip. "Which captain is tossing?"

"She can do it," says Evil Number 12. "She needs all the luck she can get."

"Honey, I was born lucky." I take the coin from the referee and rub it with my thumb and forefinger. *Luck, don't fail me now.*

The ref looks at Evil Number 12. "Call it."

I flip the coin up into the air and Evil Number 12 calls, "Heads."

I catch the falling coin and slap it onto the back of my left hand. "Tails, tails," I whisper.

"Let's see it," says the ref.

I remove my hand, and there it is. Tails up. I've won another toss. Luck is on my side.

"What do you choose?" asks the ref.

It's up to me to decide whether to kick off or to choose an end to play from. If I choose an end, then the Grizzlies get to kick off, and vice versa. Because we need any advantage we can get, we had already decided what to do if we won the toss.

"We'll kick," I say, staring Evil Number 12 right in the eye.

She frowns for a split second, but it's long enough for me to catch it.

"She knows she needs the kick advantage. She's worried about playing us. Playing me."

Evil Number 12 gives me a puzzled look. "I can hear you, you know."

"Huh?"

"Freak." She shakes her head. "We'll stay on this side," she says to the ref before running back to her position.

The ref hands me the ball and blows his whistle, and it's all down to me. I need to nail this drop kick. My strategy in times like this is to think about Jonny Wilkinson, the English fly-half. In a tied match against Australia in 2003 he received a pass and kicked a drop goal with just twenty-six seconds left to go, winning the match for England. It's probably the most famous drop kick in rugby history, and it won England the World Cup.

I take a deep breath. Time slows down. One. I take a big step forward with my right foot. Two. I take my setup step with my left foot. Three. I bounce the ball down in front of me (in rugby the ball must be bounced before you can kick it). Four. I pull my right leg back and shoot it forward from the hip as hard as I can. I'm hoping to make good contact. I'm hoping to nail that ball right down the middle of the field, nice and high so that my team can run after it. I'm hoping to get my team all the way to the touch line on our first play.

But that is not what happens. Not even close.

Chapter Six
Foul Play

My name is Lucy Graves and I am screwing up this game. The drop kick is my specialty, but this time everything goes wrong. I miscalculate the distance a little, bounce the ball too hard and put too much speed on the kick. I almost miss the ball with my foot and barely manage to kick it forward the required minimum of ten meters before it bounces again and springs back toward me. The game has been under way for less than a second, and we're already losing ground.

Evil Number 12 doesn't waste any time. She snatches up the ball and hurtles past me down the field. I spin and run after her, but she's already made headway. Like me, my teammates are in a state of momentary shock. Every second matters in a rugby game.

Evil Number 12 races past our defensive line and shakes off a feeble tackle attempt by Jenny, who fails to commit to the tackle but does get an arm hooked loosely around number 12. She's shaken off like a kitten on a Rottweiler, and she lands on her face, rolls and jumps up again to give chase. It's too late. Evil Number 12 scores a try.

It's less than a minute into the game, and we're already down five points. The pain in my stomach intensifies. "This is going to be a long eighty minutes," I say to myself. *Shut up, Lucy. Get it together.*

Andy is standing on the sideline with a shocked look on his face. He turns and places the score on the board but doesn't look back at me. Is he embarrassed for me? God, this is humiliating.

I glance at Coach. She gives a small shake of her head. Not good. Endless kicking drills are in my future for sure.

"What gives, Graves?" Emily has run up. She's pissed, and I don't blame her.

"I gashed it. I don't know. Sorry."

She sighs. "It happens," she says kindly. I wonder if I would be so kind if the situation were reversed. "But we won't let them win another point. Got it?"

"Got it."

She trots off to her position.

"I've got to come back from this. I'm the captain. My team can't see me rattled." I am openly talking to myself again, but I don't care.

My teammates look worried. Oh, how I wish I could take that terrible kick back.

The first raindrops start to fall. "Of course it's raining," I say, looking up at the sky. Normally I don't mind the rain, because it cools me off. But this field is treacherous when it's wet.

The referee blows the whistle. The Grizzlies have possession now, and they're going for a conversion. It's a tough kick for their team because they have to take it from way over by the sideline where the ball was grounded. It's hard to make a kick through the posts on that sharp of an angle. I pray they don't succeed in converting the try. Two more points that would be entirely my fault. *Please no, please no, please no.*

I hold my breath the whole time. I only let it out when the kick lands wide. *Yes.*

The game restarts with another drop kick, but this time the Grizzlies get to take it. Their kicker nails a perfect one right down the middle of our side, and the Grizzly forwards race down the field after it.

Emily snatches the ball from the air and sprints toward the oncoming Grizzlies. She sidesteps several of them like a pro and gains us some valuable ground.

The other backs and I run after her, careful to stay onside, and wait for her to either get tackled, pass the ball, chip-kick it or get all the way to the try line. As Emily runs, she can pass the ball horizontally to one of us, or she can pass it backward, but she can never pass it forward. If she even fumbled it forward, it would be considered a forward pass, or a knock-on, and we would lose possession. She's fast on her feet, and it feels good to run the field with her.

My cleats dig into the grass and dirt, and I'm thankful that I adjusted my posts last night. This field is poorly maintained and dotted with potholes, which are now filling with muddy water. Longer posts mean more traction. I run harder now because Emily is picking up speed, and I have to fight the urge to obstruct the Grizzlies coming after her. You can't block other players in rugby, and you can't tackle someone who isn't carrying the ball no matter how much you want to.

Emily's luck runs out as an oncoming Grizzly tackles her. In rugby, if you are tackled to the ground you have to release the ball. Both Emily and her attacker immediately jump up and grab at the loose ball. Another one of our teammates, a hefty lock named Samantha, leaps in to fight for possession.

The three of them have formed what's called a maul—a constantly moving, grunting, shouting, badass rugby monster. I hover close by, waiting for one of them to win the contest or for the ball to come tumbling out from between them. Just as it looks like Samantha has secured the ball and is about to break away from the maul, the opposing Grizzly prop gives her a sharp elbow to the temple.

The referee blows his whistle, and play stops. I'm hoping he's about to call for a penalty kick—it was definitely a penalty—but instead he just warns the Grizzly prop and calls for a restart. Maybe it's too early in the game to start cracking down on foul play, or maybe this referee allows for a rougher game.

As our players grumble and get in formation, I can see Evil Number 12 smirking at me. She's enjoying this. I wonder what other tricks we can expect today. The Grizzlies are fond of obstructing, punching, trampling, tripping and tackling too early or too late.

As rough as rugby is, it's supposed to be a civilized game with fair play. A lot of things get missed by the referee and the touch judges, but we can usually expect teams to keep play from getting too dangerous. I'm guilty of roughing up my opponents when the play gets heated, but I never tackle above the shoulders, and I never deliberately try to hurt anyone.

We have to restart with a scrum. A scrum is when the eight forwards of both teams join together, head-to-head, arms linked, packed down in one strange huddle. The ref places the ball into the center of the huddle, and everyone tries to get possession of the ball. The trick is that they can only use their feet and legs. The players exert incredible force on each other's necks and shoulders and heads (which is why a lot of rugby players end up with those cauliflower ears that wrestlers are famous for), and they kick and scrape their boots down each other's legs as they try to get the ball.

The scrum only ends when one team gets possession of the ball and manages to move it down the field. Sometimes that takes a few seconds. Sometimes it takes much longer.

The scrum is weird and rough and painful. As fly-half I don't join the scrum, and I'm secretly glad about that. Instead I hover around the outside of the circle, ready to act as soon as the ball emerges.

The ref blows the whistle, and the forwards link arms. I watch closely, as I have to quickly organize my defensive line if the other team gets the ball. Jessie and Lisa, our loosehead and tighthead props and the biggest members of our team, knit their strong shoulders together with those of the Grizzlies' forwards. Gina, our hooker (her job is to "hook" the ball back through the prop's legs), and Cassidy and Samantha (our two locks) join in too.

Our flankers, Jenny and Corrinne, play on the far side of the scrum from the touch line. Emily is ready to pick up the ball from the base of the scrum if it comes our way.

The scrum-half, a newer teammate of ours named Chrissy, has quick hands, but she's tiny. If I don't make sure she's protected, she's going to be meat for the Grizzlies.

Positions 11 and 14 (Wendy and Sabrina) are our wingers. They pour on the gas at the end of an attack to score tries. Positions 12 and 13 (Angel and Daya) are our centers. They stand closest to me when the backs line up. They're both strong runners with good eyes. They create space for scoring opportunities and need to be strong and powerful. Last but not least is number 15, our fullback, Ramona. It's a high-pressure position like mine that combines tackling, kicking and catching with tactical awareness.

Every one of us is on edge as the scrum comes alive. It's like a moving beast, living and breathing and steaming out on the rainy pitch.

"Come on, Eagles," I call. "You got this! Get ready!"

The other girls call out encouragement too, as does the other team. It's noisy out on the pitch.

Gina snags the ball and kicks it back through Lisa's legs. Emily snatches it up and hurtles the ball out to me horizontally in a beautiful flowing pass.

I'm already running onto the pass as she begins to throw, so I don't lose even a smidge of ground. I snatch the ball from the air and tuck it under my right arm. You're allowed to carry the ball however you want in rugby, but I prefer the one-armed carry. I use my left arm as defense and momentum. Right now I'm a juggernaut.

Chapter Seven
The Takedown

My name is Lucy Graves and I have to dig deep. My legs are pumping, my cleats are grabbing the ground, and I can feel the tightness in my calves and my quads as I push toward the other team's in-goal area. *Breathe. Breathe. Breathe.* I'm taking in so many things at once—the uneven, muddy terrain of the field, my muscles straining, my lungs burning, the rest of the team running beside and behind me, my coach calling out, spectators hooting, someone screaming, "PASS, PASS, PASS!" and the huge bodies of my opponents cutting just in front of or behind me as I sidestep and swerve around them. I'm so close to the try line. Almost there.

I see three huge Grizzlies coming at me, from all sides, and I know I've got to kick or pass. I don't want to kick, because that could be the same as giving up the ball, but at least they can't tackle me if I don't have the ball in my hands. I need to pass.

I turn my head left and right, trying to find someone to pass to. I'm outrunning my team, and it's not good. The Grizzlies almost have me.

"Lucky!" a voice shouts from the far right of the field, and I twist midstride to see Emily just on the edge of my vision. I hesitate a second too long, and if I'm honest with myself, I think it's because I don't want her to score instead of me. I do pass the ball, but I put too much force into the toss, and it just grazes the tips of her fingers before flying outside the touch line. The touch judge blows her whistle and calls the play out-of-bounds.

"Damn it, Lucy," I mutter to myself. I should have passed earlier. I know it, Emily knows it, and Coach Stevens knows it too, judging by the stinkeye she's giving me. It's a good thing there are no time-outs allowed in rugby, because I'd be on the wrong end of Coach's wrath.

When a play goes out of touch it has to be restarted by a line-out. Both teams line up opposite each other, one meter apart, and the hooker throws the ball straight down the middle of the tunnel, high above all the players. One player, usually a lock, attempts to either jump up and catch the ball or knock it back to a player on her own side. The props will help lift the jumping player by holding her up by the shorts and supporting her legs, all while avoiding contact with the other team. The player who catches the ball can keep it and fight for it in a maul, or she can pass it to a receiver. In this instance the Grizzlies will throw, because the Eagles were the last to touch the ball. If we snag it, the receiver will pass it to me. I will pass it to the back line, and we'll take off running.

The ref blows his whistle, and the Grizzlies' hooker tosses the ball. It's a perfect straight pass and the Grizzlies win possession, but Samantha tackles their scrum-half immediately and secures the ball. She shoots an awesome pass right out to me, and I turn and pass to Emily, who runs with it and passes it to Chrissy. Chrissy takes off like a tiny gazelle and immediately gets herself into a bad situation.

Chrissy has run into a pack of Grizzlies, and the rest of the team is far behind her. I am running as hard as I can to get to her, rain whipping off me, but I won't make it before a Grizzly takes her out.

As I run past the sideline, I hear Coach yell, "Tell her to kick!"

"Kick!" I scream as I run.

"Kick!" I hear Emily echo as she comes up my flank.

Out of the corner of my eye I see Andy on the sideline. He's a blur of red hair as I run past. I think I see him holding his cell phone out. Is he recording this?

Chrissy, realizing she is about to be completely murdered, stops in her tracks and looks right at me.

"Kick!" I scream again.

It's her only chance. Kicking is not a great option tactically speaking, but Chrissy is isolated and about to be pulverized. Once she kicks, she is no longer the ball carrier and can't be tackled.

"Kick!" I scream. At that exact moment Chrissy lets loose with a huge drop kick that goes straight up in the air.

"Lucky!" Emily screams. She knows she can't get there in time.

I'm already on it. I'm so close—but so is Evil Number 12. She's racing out at me from the sideline. I'm about to grab a high kick from the air, and I'm within a few yards of the Grizzlies' in-goal area. All I have to do is catch the ball before Evil Number 12 does and I can score a try. I can redeem myself. I can tie up this game and turn things around.

So close. *The ball. Get the ball.* I leap up into the air, my fingertips sensing the leather, and snatch the ball.

I feel the force of the hit even before full contact is made—before Evil Number 12 pulls an illegal move and tackles me while I'm still in the air. She's moving with such speed, and she's so heavy, that the pain reaches me before I can process what is happening.

I'm falling.

All around me, numbers fall with the raindrops. They're all the number 12.

Chapter Eight
The Zipper

My name is Lucy Graves and I am in excruciating pain. The last time my body hurt this much was when I was 12. *Number 12.* Evil Number 12 tackled me.

It was a hard hit, full speed, and she slammed her shoulder into my right hip. The tackle brought me down hard with her on top of me, all 12 million pounds of her evil muscle driving me into the soft earth of the rugby pitch, my right rugby boot planting its deep cleats into the mud. As we fell one way, my foot stayed planted. I felt my body turn the wrong way over my leg.

The sound is what haunts me now, even more than the pain of my right ankle cracking. It sounded exactly like a zipper opening, but loud enough that everyone on the field heard it. Even the people on the sidelines must have heard it, because it seems like I've only been on the ground for a few moments when I see my mom's face hovering over me. There's Coach, and Emily, and even Evil Number 12, who looks like she's going to throw up.

Someone keeps saying, "Oh my god, oh my god." I think it's me.

I look up at Mom, at the worry on her face, framed by the raining sky, and a flash takes me back to when I was 12. When Dad looked at me exactly the same way. The last time I was in this much pain. The last time I was this scared. The last time I saw him alive.

Don't be scared, baby. Daddy's here. Everything is going to be okay. You're my lucky charm...my Lucy...my lucky...

"Lucy!" Mom's voice cuts through, and the gray image of my father dissolves.

"She passed out again," says Coach Stevens.

I look up at my mom, trying to focus, but she keeps slipping into a black shadow. My dad's face appears again, and everything goes white until the raindrops wake me up.

"I'm sorry, I'm so sorry," a teenage girl is crying somewhere behind me.

I turn my head and vomit, and that's when my mom goes into action. I hear her calling 9-1-1, trying hard to disguise the panic in her voice.

"I'm sorry, Daddy. I'm so sorry." Why won't that girl stop crying?

"Lucy," says Emily, hovering over my face. "It's going to be okay."

I try to push her hand off my shoulder, but I feel so weak. Just lifting my arm sends a shock wave of pain down my leg. I fall into blackness again.

Dad is with me. It's snowing. But there's a strange orange glow. My neck hurts so much. Daddy...

Chapter Nine

Flirting With Disaster

My name is Lucy Graves and I am injured.
When I wake up I'm on a stretcher being unloaded into the hospital's ambulance bay. We bump against the curb, and I cry out in pain. The whole world seems to flood back in bright relief. Wow, I am definitely awake now.

"Oh great," I say, as the paramedics wheel me through the doors. "I wake up just in time to wait in agonizing pain. For hours, I'm sure." I've been in this ER before, mainly for stitches, and it takes forever.

"It always amazes me the capacity a teenager has for sarcasm, even in emergent situations," says one paramedic to the other. She's got wild blond hair and kind eyes. I like her immediately.

"Really, Susan," jokes the other paramedic in return. "You should write a bestselling book about that so you can stop wheeling their whiny butts into emerg every day." He looks down at me and gives me a wink.

I chuckle, but it hurts so bad that a tear rolls down my cheek.

"It's okay, honey," says Susan. "You're not going to have to wait too long. The benefit of rolling in with us is you get looked at sooner."

"Yay." My voice is weak, and I can feel bile rising in my throat.

As we roll in, the bright lights don't help. I wince at the glare, my head pounding. I do have to wait a little while, so to distract myself I start listing all the famous rugby injuries I can recall.

RIGHTEOUS RUGBY INJURIES

1. Jharal Yow Yeh of the Brisbane Broncos suffered a nightmarish broken ankle.
2. Beau Robinson of the Queensland Reds dislocated his elbow after his arm got twisted in a knot.
3. Martin Groenewald of South Africa cracked his leg in two places live on TV.
4. Lachine Munro of Lyon ripped his bottom lip completely in half.
5. Alexandre Dumoulin of France lost the tip of his nose.
6. Kiwi Shaun Kenny-Dowall played a game with a fractured jaw.
7. Sam McKendry broke his neck but kept on playing.

Weirdly, my gory list is helping with the pain. I see my mom hurrying in.

"Lucy, baby, how are you?" Her brows are pushed together, and she looks green with worry.

"I'm okay, I think," I lie, but I can't handle the look on Mom's face. I've seen it before, and it's bringing back terrible memories.

"Oh, honey. I'm so sorry. How's your head? Do you feel sick? How's your pain?"

"Mom, chill. It's not a big deal. I'm not that hurt. I just got my bell rung and twisted my ankle. I'll be fine. They'll probably just poke me a few times and send me on my way with my own special tensor bandage. You know the drill. They'll just tell me to RICE it."

THE RICE TECHNIQUE FOR SPORT INJURIES

1. Rest
2. Ice
3. Compress
4. Elevate

I've been hurt playing rugby before. It isn't the first time and won't be the last.

"Yeah," says Mom, trying to smile. "I know you're tough."

"Let's see what's going on here, shall we?" A tall wiry doctor with an accent I can't quite place steps into my curtained area while reading my chart, closes it and pulls up a chair. He looks me deep in the eyes and immediately puts me at ease.

"I'm Dr. Connell," he says.

Got it. "New Zealand?" I ask.

"Why, yes. You know your accents, do you?" He seems surprised.

"Just meeting a lot of you Kiwis lately," I say. Oh no. Andy saw my spectacular rugby fail.

"Well," says Dr. Connell, "one good thing about having a Kiwi doctor when you've been hurt during a rugby battle is that you can rest assured I've been there too. A few times." He winks.

Are all Kiwis flirts? I look over at Mom, and she's grinning at him and twirling her long hair around her finger. Barf.

"And"—he nods at my right foot—"I know how to take off a rugby boot when you've had a cracker like this one."

"No way. Please don't take it off." I try to scoot farther back on the bed, but the pain stops me.

"Sorry. Have to," he says. "Need X-rays. No way around it, I'm afraid."

I shudder as he begins pulling the laces. He is slow and meticulous, and I can tell he's trying hard not to cause me any more pain. When he gets ready to slide the boot off, Mom winces, and I grab on to her hand for support.

"Okay, Lucy. Deep breath," he says. "You're a rugby player. Toughen up."

"Right," I say, but I'm not feeling too tough.

I breathe in, and he slips off the boot. A burning pain shoots up the back of my ankle and into my shin. It feels like someone is stabbing me with a hot metal rod.

"Ah!" I cry out. "Please, please don't touch it again!"

"Okay," he says. "I'm going to send you for your X-ray, but I just want to check you over a bit first."

He proceeds to gently place his hands up and down my legs and my arms and along my neck and shoulders. He softly palpates my abdomen and taps on it, listening. He carefully looks in my eyes and ears and asks me several questions about my day. We talk about rugby stats, and by the end of it I'm actually getting irritated. I am in serious pain here, and this guy wants to talk about the weather and what I had for lunch.

Satisfied that I'm not going to die immediately, he turns to my mother. She perks up right away.

"Mrs. Graves," he begins.

"Ms.," she corrects him. "But you can call me Amanda."

If I rolled my eyes any harder, they'd pop right out of my head.

"Right." He smiles. "Amanda, I don't think Lucy has suffered a serious head injury. It seems like a mild concussion at most. The loss of consciousness and the vomiting are a concern, but they have subsided, and I don't see any other deficits or signs of trauma. I think we can observe her for a while, and then you'll need to keep close watch on her overnight to ensure there are no issues. You don't need to wake her every couple of hours—we don't do that anymore because we need to let the injured brain rest and heal—but I do want you to bring her back here right away if her condition changes. If she shows signs of confusion or starts vomiting again, she needs to be reassessed."

"Okay," Mom says. "That's a relief. But I should mention—" She hesitates, looking at me. "She does have a history. I mean, she was in a very serious car accident when she was 12, and the girl who landed on her today was so big."

"Mom!" I interject. I look at the doctor. "I'm fine. I have an old injury to my neck, but I had surgery and it's healed. My head hurts a bit, but the only thing I care about right now is my leg. I just need ice. And maybe a tensor."

"Baby." Mom reaches out to stroke my hair, but I swat her hand away.

"Lucy," says Dr. Connell, "I doubt a tensor will help. But we can cross our fingers."

"What do you mean? Are you saying it's broken?" I don't like the way this conversation is going.

"I'm saying we do need an X ray. But there is a downside to having a Kiwi rugby-playing doctor. I know a broken leg when I see one."

Chapter Ten
Out Of Luck

My name is Lucy Graves and I cannot have a broken leg. I just can't. A nurse wheels me to radiology, where an X-ray technician tortures my ankle into various positions. Afterward I languish in the ER with Mom as we wait for the results. All I can do is try to swallow the lump that has formed in my throat. It feels like it's going to choke me to death. I make lists in my mind to distract me from the pain.

THINGS I'M AFRAID OF

1. Spiders. Ew.
2. Car accidents, obviously.
3. Fire.
4. Bad tackles gone wrong.
5. Breaking a leg.

THINGS PEOPLE SAY
THAT MAKE ME CRAZY

1. "It's not the end of the world." Really? How do they know? MAYBE IT IS.
2. "There's no such thing as bad luck." My (probably broken) leg begs to differ. Right now I feel straight-up cursed.
3. "Relax." I really don't understand this one. How is everyone else so calm all the time? I'm barely hanging on. Don't they know it's pretty much guaranteed that their safe little bubble is going to burst at any moment? How do other people get through each day without letting the fear overtake them? It's exhausting—all the pretending and acting like everything is just hunky-dory.

No, everything is definitely not fine. When Dr. Connell comes back into my curtained area and pulls back the thin green fabric, I can tell the news is not good. I've seen that look on a doctor's face before.

My ankle is broken. I listen vaguely as Dr. Connell talks to mom, but they both seem like they're floating off in a fog. I can't deal with this anymore.

"The break isn't displaced," says Dr. Connell, his voice echoing. "The talus hasn't moved out of its proper position, and the fracture itself is small."

"How can something so small cause so much pain?" I wonder aloud.

"I know you can't even see it on the X-ray," says Dr. Connell, "but the tissues surrounding your ankle are damaged. It's going to take time and physiotherapy to heal. At minimum you'll need to be on crutches, with a special boot, for a couple weeks, and then you'll have to do as much physio and rehab as you can handle if you want to play rugby again this season."

If I want to play. "*If* I want to play?" My voice comes out in a strangled squeak, and Mom reaches out to place her hand on my shoulder.

"Here's the name of a good physiotherapist." Dr. Connell hands Mom a card. Then he sits down next to me and looks me in the eye. "Lucy, I promise you will get back to rugby eventually. But we will have to see how your body responds to the physio. Don't push it too hard too soon. I don't want you to make it worse. I hear you have a reputation for pushing it." He looks over at Mom, who smiles.

"Don't worry," I say. "It hurts so bad right now, I can't imagine standing on it, let alone running or kicking."

I leave the hospital with a nifty pair of crutches, a black Darth Vader boot thing and a prescription for painkillers, which I most definitely will not take. I don't like medicine, and I'd rather feel the pain. Pain means I'm alive.

But as I struggle to transfer from the hospital's wheelchair to my mom's Civic,

I can't help but wonder if this kind of pain is going to be too much for me. Something about Dr. Connell's promise worries me. Because if I'm honest, I'm scared that more than my leg got broken on the field today. Somewhere out there in the mud is my rugby career. My future. My freedom.

Chapter Eleven
Aftermath

My name is Lucy Graves and I am trapped.
I'm sitting in the Civic in the rain while Mom brings stuff from the car to our townhouse.

"If I can't play rugby, what am I going to do with my life?" I ask out loud. But there is no answer save for the pattering rain.

Mom comes to help me out of the car. I can manage on the crutches, but every time I hop forward, my injured leg gets jostled. Clenching my teeth in agony, I take what seems like hours to hobble up our short walkway and the three concrete stairs that lead into our place. By the time I get inside I'm drenched in sweat.

I'm still wearing my rugby uniform, but I can't imagine crutching all the way to my room at the back of the house to change. Instead I thank the gods for sectional couches and make myself as comfortable as possible on the nearest corner of the sofa. The fabric is a soft microsuede, and I remember helping my mom assemble it. I start to cry as I think of all the things I won't be able to help her with now.

Mom comes out of the kitchen with a glass of water and my pain pills. When she sees me crying, she rushes over.

"Lucy, honey. Is it the pain?"

I shake my head. I feel like I can't breathe. "My chest hurts," I choke out.

"Lucy, baby, you've got to calm down. Let me help you. Please." Mom tries to get me to focus, but it's not working.

"I can't. I can't."

"Can't what, honey?"

"I can't," I repeat. It's like I'm stuck and don't have any other words. I want to tell her I can't calm down. That I can't stop thinking about the number 12, and I can't help her with anything around the house, and I can't manage on these crutches, and I can't play rugby, and I can't imagine what life will be like now. I can't say any of this to her. All I keep thinking about is the number 12.

"Drink this." She offers me the water.

I take it from her and gulp it down. It hurts as it travels down my throat and into my stomach. It feels like there's a huge ball stuck right behind my chest wall.

My vision is grainy, like I might pass out, and the pain in my chest intensifies. *Oh my god, am I having a heart attack?* I hear a strange whooshing sound in my ears, and I realize to my horror that it is the sound of my heart pounding. It's going crazy fast, and I feel like at any moment I will hear it stop. *Did my heart just skip a beat? Two beats?* Now it feels like it's thumping out of control. I clutch at my chest with one hand and drop the water glass onto the carpet. I reach out and grab Mom's arm in desperation.

"Mom," I manage. "It's happening... again."

Mom ignores the dropped glass and gets up to turn out the lights. She sits down next to me, wraps her arms around me and holds me so tight that I can't feel myself shaking.

"Everything is okay. You are going to be fine. This is a panic attack." She repeats the same few sentences.

"Breathe, Lucy. Breathe," she instructs.

At first it's impossible, terrifying, and I feel like I'm going to die at any moment. As I breathe and focus on my mom's voice, my heart rate slows and the violent shaking calms.

THINGS THAT HELP
DURING A PANIC ATTACK
1. Dimmed lights.
2. Being wrapped up tight.

3. Being reminded that I am not dying, that I will be okay.

After a few minutes I feel well enough to ask for more water.

Mom sits across from me, her face a storm of concern. "Lucy," she says. "You haven't had a panic attack since—"

"Since I was 12," I finish for her.

My lucky charm...

Dad's voice in my mind again. That bad hit on the field and the shock of the injury is opening up wounds I want to keep in the past. I don't have time to spiral out of control again.

"I've got to get better. I've got to get back to my team. I've got to get a scholarship." I feel the pressure rising in my chest again.

"Listen," says Mom. "You will be fine. Right now you need to just focus on healing. Everything will work out."

But I can't help thinking about school and rugby and scholarships, and my heart starts to race again. I reach for my trusty rugby ball but realize it isn't here.

"Mom, where's my ball? Oh my god, I lost my lucky rugby ball!"

"It's okay. I remembered to grab it," she says. "I know how important it is to you." She looks at me sadly for a moment. It must be hard for her to look at that old thing.

"It's in the back of the car," she adds. "I'll go get it."

"Thanks, Mom."

As she gets up I notice three figures walk past our front window. Mom opens the door and ushers them in as she goes out to fetch my ball.

Coach Stevens comes in first, looking worried and exhausted.

Then Emily appears—she's still wearing her muddy rugby gear too.

The third person comes in, and my heart leaps into my throat again. It's Andy Williams, Mr. Princely Redhead himself.

Chapter Twelve
Misery Loves Company

My name is Lucy Graves and I am going to kill Emily Jones. I mean, I've been CRYING and somehow Andy Williams is walking INTO MY LIVING ROOM. Did I mention that he's carrying FLOWERS? I stare at him. He's all freckly and smiling and looking right at me, and I am going to KILL Emily for bringing him here and not even giving me a heads-up. I mean, I've been CRYING.

Coach approaches, clearing her throat and shifting her weight from foot to foot.

"Hey, Lucy," she says. "How's the leg? How's your head? You doing okay? I'm really sorry this happened."

She's fairly gruff at the best of times, and right now she seems way out of her element. I prefer Coach when she's barking orders and being a total boss. Sympathetic Coach is kind of alarming. And a bit annoying.

"Uh, well, not great," I answer. I point to my ankle. "Broken."

"No!" says Emily, a bit too loudly and dramatically for my taste. She reaches for Andy and clutches his arm.

I feel my stomach clench as a surge of rage rushes through me, but I keep it together when I see Andy take a small step back from Emily.

"Geez, Emily," I snarl. "What are you, a Southern belle?"

Andy winces.

"Lucy!" Mom is standing in the doorway.

Great—she came back just in time to hear my awful comment.

"Sorry," I mutter. "I'm not feeling too great."

"We won't stay," says Coach.

"We just wanted to see how you were doing," says Andy in a soft voice. He hands me the flowers. It's a small bouquet of daisies. Emily must have told him they're my favorite. I'm such a jerk.

"Thanks," I manage.

"Lucy," says Emily, "we wanted you to know what happened with the game."

The game. Of course, the game. It's not as if the game would have ended just because I got hurt. The play would have continued.

I look at them and try to act interested. "Don't keep me in suspense, Jones."

"We won!" says Emily, giving a little hop.

"Great," I say, but my voice is grim. Mom gives me another one of her looks.

Emily continues, unfazed. "Well, after you...you know...the ref called a penalty kick, and we scored!"

"Who took the kick?" I ask.

"I did," says Emily, her smile faltering a little.

I nod. "Makes sense. But wait—who played fly-half?"

Coach chimes in. "We got Candace Peters in there."

"Candace?" I ask. "She's been riding the bench all season. And she's a prop!"

"I know," says Emily. "But she makes a decent fly-half. Nowhere near as good as you, of course," she adds quickly. "Turns out she's got a pretty decent passing game."

"Emily, you're being modest," says Andy. Then, to me, he adds, "Emily scored three times."

Emily shrugs and looks at her feet.

"Wow," I say. "Good job, Jones."

"I did it for you, Lucky," Emily says, her eyes wide and sincere.

I can't bring myself to thank her. It's great that we won, and I am happy for Emily, but I'm dying inside.

I try to swallow, but my mouth has gone so dry that I cough. "What happened to Evil Number 12?" I ask.

Mom gives me a questioning look.

"Who?" asks Coach.

"The Grizzly who sacked me," I explain.

"She got ejected from the game," says Andy. "Good riddance too," he adds. "She was a...big meanie." He gives me a silly smile, and I can tell he's trying to lighten the mood and make me feel better.

Mom offers everyone something to drink, but they say they have to go, noting how tired I look and the fact that there's school tomorrow.

Coach and Emily leave first, and I'm kind of relieved that Andy isn't getting a ride home with Emily. I don't like the idea of them alone together at all.

Andy sits down next to me and points to my leg. "So you couldn't even get a proper cast?"

"What?" I ask.

"Well, how am I supposed to sign that thing?" he asks. "It's not plaster and it's black."

"Welcome to the future," I say, and I swear he giggles.

"I'm sorry you got hurt." He's so sincere that I want to kiss him, but my mom is hovering at the edge of the living room.

"Thanks," I say. "I can handle it."

"Well, I'm sort of glad in a way—not that you're hurt, but that you will need to recover. You need to take time for yourself now. And I'm quite good at that."

He bumps me with his shoulder a little too hard, but I don't mind. Not at all.

"You're good at taking time?" I ask.

"Yeah. You know, chilling. I can bring you things. And I can take you places. I've got a car. I can buy you ice cream."

"Ice cream?"

I notice his knee is shaking a little. He's so adorably nervous.

"Or popcorn. Like at the movies. Sort of like a date."

"Sort of?"

"Exactly," he says. "Exactly like a date." He looks at me with warm eyes.

It's just the sweetest thing anyone's said to me in a long time. I can feel myself almost starting to cry, so I try to find a way to hurry him out the door.

"Okay," I say. "Sure, we can go on a date."

"Yeah?" He seems surprised.

"Yeah. But I'm tired now. I need to rest."

He jumps to his feet. "Of course. I'll call you. Emily gave me your number. She's quite nice, isn't she?"

"Yes." I nod. "She is. She's a much better person than I am."

He chuckles, thinking I'm making a joke.

"Okay, kids," Mom says, stepping back into the room. "Time to say goodnight."

"Goodnight," says Andy, and he kind of bows his head.

"Bye," I say, noting that he really is rather prince-like.

After Mom sees him out she tries to get me to go back to my room to sleep, but I'm too exhausted. I beg her for a blanket and reluctantly swallow half a painkiller. Eventually I fall asleep reclining on the coach. It's a heavy, fitful sleep, broken by Mom sneaking up to check on me, and I have terrible dreams all night long.

I am 12. The snow is falling. My neck hurts. What is that bright-orange glow? Don't leave me, Daddy. Please don't leave me...

Chapter Thirteen
Going Viral

My name is Lucy Graves and I am a cautionary tale. During the next week at home I sleep a lot and deal with the burning pain, the nightmares and the anxiety. I eat a lot too, which makes Mom happy.

Andy calls every day to see how I am, and every time he calls, Mom smiles when she answers. She's started referring to him as "that thoughtful boy"—a parental dream so far.

Emily sends me text messages and emails me my homework, and Mr. McCabe leaves a voice mail wishing me well and asking me to reconsider Mathletes. He's relentless.

Without my usual breakneck schedule, I finally have time to indulge in some serious viewing of my collection of recorded rugby "sevens" games. Rugby sevens is like regular rugby but the squads are made up of seven players, and they play seven-minute halves. The rugby I play requires fifteen players and forty-minute halves.

I also review my own tapes—recordings of my highlights compiled into a reel so I can include them with my scholarship applications. I'm supposed to send them directly to the coaches of the colleges I want to attend. My reel is heavy on the kicks. I specialize in them all.

SOME OF MY FAVORITE RUGBY KICKS

1. The touch finder (when you kick directly to the touch area from behind your own 22-meter line)

2. The box kick (great in a high-pressure situation)
3. The up-and-under, or Garryowen (risky but worth it)
4. The chip and chase (a last-resort kick that results in a chase)
5. The cross field (switches the direction of the attack)

After a few days of nonstop rugby viewing, I'm starting to feel not-so-terrible about life. Then Emily texts me a link along with a message.

You've gone viral!

I hesitate for a second before tapping it.

It's a YouTube video that someone has titled "Chick Rugby Blooper." The clip is an endless loop of me being tackled in spectacular fashion. Not the best highlight reel.

The title is what burns me the most. *Blooper* is a ridiculous word for the exact moment when my whole life cracked in half. But whatever. It's also set to silly carnival music, which makes my injury look comical—until the moment when my leg twists the wrong way.

A quick scroll through the comment section reveals a range of teenage sensitivity.

TOP YOUTUBE COMMENTS

1. *Dude, I know that chick.*
2. *Whoa! Sick!*
3. *This is why girls shouldn't play guy sports.*
4. *This is kind of hot.*
5. *Gross!*
6. *LOL. FAIL.*

I turn the sound off and click the video to watch it again. The cruelest part of the clip isn't my leg breaking. It's my dazed face rising from the dirt. I look so wounded. I play it again. I watch it 12 times. Then 12 more. I keep it loaded on my home screen so I can play it constantly.

Mom knocks on my door. I turn off my phone before saying, "Come in." She doesn't ever need to see this.

"Good to see you back in your room, kiddo."

"What's up?" I ask, motioning to the box.

"I'm working tonight," she says. "Will you be okay on your own?"

"I'll be fine," I say. "I need to catch up on math anyway."

"Hey, why don't you call that cute redhead?" she asks with a wink.

"Mom!"

"What?"

"Don't say *cute redhead*."

"Why? He is cute. And he's so thoughtful."

"Okay," I say. "That's enough. I will call him. Okay? Now go. You've accomplished everything on your twisted Mom-to-do list."

After she's gone I pick up my phone, fighting the urge to watch the video again. I find Andy's number, hesitate for a moment, then press the Call button.

It rings once before he answers. He sounds muffled.

"Hello?" I ask. "Andy? I can't hear you."

"Lucy," he whispers. "I'm hiding."

"Hiding? Are you okay?"

"Yeah, I'm just hiding out from my brother," he says. "He's kind of...annoying. Can I come over?"

"Yeah, sure," I say. "Bring food."

A half hour later Andy is in my living room, and he's brought a feast. Burgers, sushi, tacos.

"I didn't know what you like," he says.

"I like everything!" I say. "So this is awesome."

We talk about math, movies, teachers we don't like and the cheesy plaques on Mr. McCabe's walls at school. It's easy and comfortable and the most fun I've had in a while.

Between courses of delicious grub, Andy pulls out a small white sticky label and rubs it onto the side of my big dorky boot. He takes out a red felt marker and signs his name.

"Are you claiming me or something?" I tease.

He looks deeply into my eyes, a soft smile on his face. "I wouldn't dare."

I quickly change the subject and ask him about moving here from New Zealand. He fidgets with the cuff of his sweater, pulling at the loose threads.

"It's, you know, kind of lonely, I guess." He gives me a silly grin, so I can't be sure if he's joking or not.

"Well, I wouldn't know. I've never been anywhere."

"It's overrated," he says. "My parents like to move around a lot, change things up. Seems like they're looking for something to distract them from their crappy marriage. Total cliché. It's a drag not staying in one place for very long."

Andy flashes that same silly grin again, and I can see that it's something he does when he's scared of getting too real. It only makes me like him more.

"So if you had your way, you'd stay?" I ask, suddenly feeling shy.

He scoots a little closer to me on the couch.

"If I had my way, I would never leave. I'd be like that old guy from the movie who refuses to sell his house, you know? They'd be building all around me and I'd just stay."

"Andy Williams, are you trying to tell me you're stubborn?" I jostle him with my elbow.

He laughs. "Maybe. But also I just really hate packing." He reaches over and moves a stray piece of hair away from my face. His eyes take on a faraway look. "Sometimes I get the feeling my family wouldn't care if I just...forgot to come with them next time."

"What do you mean?" I ask.

"I don't know, never mind. I'm in a weird mood, I guess."

"What about your brother?" I ask, hoping a change in subject will help. "You said he was annoying."

Andy nods. "He's a couple years older. He's a lot like my dad. He kind of likes to pick on people. Especially me."

"Oh," I say, because I don't know what else to say.

"It's okay," he says. "It could be worse. I could have a broken ankle."

He smiles at me.

"Low blow, Red," I say.

"Red?" he asks, raising an eyebrow. "So I've been reduced to a hair color now, have I? Well, at least you didn't call me Ginger."

"No," I say. "I'm not teasing you. I mean, I'm not making fun of you. I like it. I like your red hair. I like you."

He looks at me, and his expression is soft and open. He leans over to kiss me, and all I can think of are the bites of cheeseburger, spicy tuna roll, the taco with extra-hot sauce. But as soon as the softness of his lips brush against mine, I forget all of that. When we finally pull apart, my heart is pounding.

Andy picks up another taco and takes a big messy bite, bits of lettuce and sauce falling onto his chin. I laugh and do the same.

We don't have to say it, but we're together. Andy, the redheaded prince, and me, the unlucky rugby player. It's funny how good things come on the heels of the bad. Fingers crossed that it doesn't work the other way around.

Chapter Fourteen
Offside

My name is Lucy Graves and I am a sucker for redheads. I didn't know this about myself, but I like being someone's girlfriend. I'm sweet on Andy. Yes, I know how gross that sounds. Pre-broken-ankle-me would have hated that.

We've been spending so much time together that Mom probably regrets pushing me to call him. He's always over at the house, pretending to work on math, and since I started back at school he's been giving me rides in his beat-up Volvo.

School is fine. It's bearable, but it's hard to ignore the stares. There's always some moron who thinks they need to show me that video, as if I don't remember every second.

All that time stuck at home means I'm caught up on schoolwork, and I've managed to ditch the crutches. I'm still wearing the big boot for support, but I started physio yesterday. The therapist, a fit and wiry woman named Connie, was merciless as she pushed my ankle through its range of motion. Because I'm an athlete and I was strong and flexible before my injury, I should also be able to heal faster. That's good news. I still need to work on my dorsal and plantar flex. I've been given special bands to do my stretches with, and Connie told me I should try swimming to help build up strength and flexibility.

Today I'm planning on going to a rugby game after school. I won't be able to play for a while yet, but there's no reason I can't support my team. Today they're playing the Lincoln Lions, a team from a few towns over. The Eagles and the Lions are pretty evenly matched. By the time I get done with some last-minute math homework and hobble out to the field, the game is under way and already tied.

Emily leads the team in spreading the play wide across the field. She chucks a tough pass to Jenny, who hangs on but is taken over the sideline. After the line-out, Emily makes a break through the middle and scores a try. We're up five points! Candace manages to convert the goal, and we get two more points. Now we're up seven and winning the game.

Unfortunately, we lose possession of the ball in a handling error, and a scrum is formed. We win the ball in the scrum and manage to get it to Emily, who just stays onside. Once again she pours on the gas and scores another try. We don't get the conversion this time, but it doesn't matter because our team is on fire. Being up so many points is a huge confidence booster, and we keep running away with the ball. Emily dives into a corner to score another try.

Time runs out, and the Eagles win. Even though I didn't play, it's still exciting, and it means our team is that much closer to going to the championships.

The team is huddled together around Emily, giving her praise. I decide to suck it up and go over to join in.

As I approach the group they break apart, and I see that Coach Stevens is handing Emily a new jersey. It's Emily's number 8, but it has a new symbol on it. Where there used to be an *A* for "assistant captain," there is now a *C*.

Just like that, I've been replaced.

My name is Lucy Graves and I have been betrayed. I can't be captain anymore because I got hurt? I made this team what it is. No one even has the nerve to look me in the eye. Emily begins to stammer out an explanation, but I don't give her a chance. I just hobble out of there as fast as I can.

Andy meets me in the parking lot, but I'm so mad I can't even sit in his car when he opens the door for me. I pace back and forth with one hand on the car for support while he stares at me. I can't stop ranting.

"Screw this! If Emily thinks she's going to take over, she's out of her mind." I feel like screaming.

"Lucy," says Andy in a gentle tone. "I don't think that's the right approach to solving this problem." He's so annoyingly reasonable sometimes.

"Oh no? Just watch. I'm going to rehab my ankle. I'm getting back in the game. I can't let any more time go by. I'm nothing without rugby."

"That's nonsense. You have your academics. You have your mom. You have me."

I ignore him. "It's all about rugby. From now on I'm a machine. Cue the *Rocky* montage. The getting-busy part."

"The what?" He looks at me. "Getting... busy? Like..." He leans in closer and says in a low, sexy whisper, "Busy?"

I swat his shoulder. "Get your mind out of the gutter! Not that kind of getting busy. I mean the getting-busy part," I say again.

He stares at me blankly and shrugs his shoulders.

"You know. The montage," I say. "Whenever there's a setback in a sports movie, there's ultimately a time when the hero steps up his game—or her game, in this case—and gets busy. Like, busy."

"Oh," he says, kind of disappointed. "Wait. You mean like when Rocky is lifting logs and punching meat and stuff? Eye of the tiger?"

"Yeah! You know your *Rocky* movies!"

"So you want to punch meat?"

"Yes! No. Just metaphorically. I have to train. Hard."

"I can help you," he says. "I can analyze your stats, your output, your progress, and help you design a program to get you out there faster." He starts pacing too, excited now.

"That's so cute," I say.

"What?"

"You're using math to help me with sports."

"So I'm like your trainer then, right?"

"Don't push it."

"No, seriously, I'm like Mickey. The old trainer dude?"

I laugh. "No, babe, you're my Adrian."

"Okay, I'll take it," he says. "Cue the music."

We get into his car and head straight for the gym.

Chapter Fifteen
Eye Of The Tiger

My name is Lucy Graves and I will not give in. Andy wasn't kidding when he said he would help with the getting-busy plan. He comes up with a complicated spreadsheet with all kinds of workout data. It's an intense regimen, so I condensed it into a list, as I do.

THE WORK-OUT-UNTIL-YOU-BARF PLAN

1. Go to physio and get ultrasound treatments.

2. Endure painful stretches and massages.
3. Hit up the sauna and do hydrotherapy.
4. Swim endless laps with a kickboard (while Andy lounges in the hot tub).
5. Lift light weights, lift heavy weights, and do body-weight exercises until I barf.
6. Yoga, yoga, yoga.

It feels amazing to be working out hard again. When I'm swimming I zone out and get into a rhythm with my breathing. I love pulling myself through the water and feeling my muscles stretch and contract with every kick and stroke. The buoyancy and resistance of the warm water is comforting, and I love how the rest of the world just falls away while I revel in what my body can do. Each exercise brings me closer to feeling like my old self again.

For inspiration before my workouts, I watch the New Zealand Black Ferns perform their haka dance pregame ritual. It's a traditional war dance used by the Maori culture in order to terrify and intimidate their opponents. Let me tell you, it works. Seeing a team of tough female rugby players all stomping, chanting and making wild faces really gets my blood going.

After he sets up the exercise component, Andy turns his laser focus to food.

THE EAT-ALL-THE-THINGS PLAN
1. Start the day with a green smoothie.
2. Scarf a protein shake every three hours.
3. Choke down endless citrus fruits (for tissue regeneration).
4. Eat until I can't eat anymore.

And just when I think Andy might be getting a bit too into this whole trainer thing, he adds in some fun by taking me to one of those indoor kids' play places with the big climbing structures. But when he tries to get me onto the huge trampoline, I freak out.

"No. Way!" I shriek as I watch a horde of little kids throwing themselves around on the bouncy surface. "Do you want me to bust my ankle again?"

"You have to get over this," Andy says. "You're strong. Your doctor and physiotherapist say it's time to push it. After all, how can you play a game if you can't even jump on a trampoline?"

He's right. Some gentle bouncing and rebounding would be a lot less stressful to my ankle joint than playing rugby.

"Fine. But I blame you if one of these rug rats takes me out."

"Deal," Andy says, stepping out onto the huge trampoline with me. "Now let's bounce."

The two of us spend the next half hour gently bouncing up and down, until it feels less scary. I get tired and my leg is hurting, so Andy treats me to a demonstration of his trampoline tricks. Apparently he had a brief but dazzling period as a child gymnast. He's all elbows and knees as he leaps in the air and does bum drops and spins. It's hilarious.

Tomorrow I'm planning to attend rugby running practice, which is when my team practices drills and passing. I'm not sure I'll be ready for the running or for facing Emily as captain, but as I watch Andy gleefully flail in the air, I think I might be able to handle it. I hope I can.

Chapter Sixteen
Spiraling

My name is Lucy Graves and I am losing it. By the time I get to running practice after school I am seriously on edge. It doesn't help that I'm nervous about putting on cleats again. What if I roll my ankle? Twist it? Step in a pothole?

When I walk onto the field, I try to ignore the twinge in my ankle and the awkward glances from my teammates.

Emily jogs up to me. "Hey, Lucy," she says. "I just wanted to—"

"Save it," I say, cutting her off. "I'm just here to run."

"Oh. That's great. You're ready to do that already? Is your leg–"

"It's fine. Perfect, actually. Never better." I give her a tight smile and start doing some light stretches.

Coach looks over at me and gives me a nod. "Good to have you back, Lucy. Just do what you can, okay?"

"I'm good, Coach. I'm ready."

"Okay," says Coach. "Lines!" She blows her whistle, and the team starts running across the middle of the field.

We need to run up and touch each line on the field and then return to the start, going back and forth as fast as we can, endlessly. It sucks. I'm normally pretty good at it, because I'm one of the taller and faster players, but I quickly find that I'm struggling to keep up.

I'm afraid to pour on my full speed because of the short, quick stops on each line. What if I jam my ankle? Everyone on the team finishes before me, but I ignore Coach when she tries to end my torture early. I complete all the lines in my own time and trot over for a break.

"Graves," says Coach. "When I call you out, just come."

I shrug. She's not my favorite person right now.

Coach gives me a look, but I brush it off.

"Okay, ladies," she says. "Time for some takedowns and tackles."

Is she serious?

Emily gives me a look of concern.

"Tackles?" I ask, my voice quiet.

"We've all gotten a bit sloppy out there," says Coach. "We need to practice tackling and get used to being tackled. Safely," she adds.

"But..." Emily trails off, giving me a look of pity that boils my blood.

"Lucy, are you feeling up for it?" asks Coach.

Is she challenging me? Coach isn't above pushing me to my limits, but now? This?

"Bring it," I throw back, and I jog over to take my spot in the lineup on the field.

During tackle practice we form two lines, each flanked by a single player. One player from each line runs forward with the ball, and the flanking player tackles them and goes to the back of the line to take their turn. The tackled player gets up and becomes the tackler. This repeats over and over until we can barely stand up.

A good rugby tackle takes out the ball carrier in the field of play, but they're only considered tackled if you can hold them and bring them to the ground. Coach teaches us that just getting one knee down can be enough to count, so it doesn't have to be dramatic. But you have to let the tackled player go right away, and you can't play the ball until you're on your feet too. The really tricky part is trying not to obstruct the other team when you're getting tackled. I mean, sometimes you just cannot control your body position.

I'm near the back of the line, and by the time my turn comes around I'm a wreck.

It turns out that Emily is to be my tackler. I hope she makes a clean hit. If she hesitates it could be awkward, and we could get more hurt than if she just does a good takedown.

The ball gets tossed to me, and I take a deep breath, running forward with my head up and eyes forward. Out of the corner of my eye I see the royal blue of Emily's jersey and feel her weight wrap around my waist as she slams into me. It's a hard hit, harder than we normally practice. My breath rushes out of me as she lands on me.

"What the hell, Emily!" I shout, sitting up. "Are you trying to hurt me?"

"I-I'm sorry, Lucky," she stammers.

"Don't call me that!"

"I'm sorry. I was nervous. I overthought the tackle and put too much speed on it. I was trying to be careful."

"Yeah, well, next time spare me your concern," I snap.

"Hey!" Coach Steven yells out. "What's the problem, Graves?"

"You saw what she did!" I am yelling back at her now, so mad my vision starts to blur. "She's trying to hurt me."

"Why would I do that?" Emily asks.

"Because you don't want the competition," I say. "You only got that C on your chest by default, you know."

"Lucy, that is enough," says Coach.

"I bet you put out that video too, didn't you?" I ask Emily. I feel like all the pain and frustration and hurt of the last several weeks is finally about to burst, but I also feel close to losing it completely. "You were the one who sent me the 'viral' link."

"What?" Emily shrieks. "You're paranoid."

"Do you deny it?"

"Why don't you ask your boyfriend about it," she says coldly.

I follow her gaze to the bleachers. Andy is standing up, watching our drama unfold. I feel sick to my stomach. *What is happening?*

"What is that supposed to mean?" I ask.

Emily just shakes her head.

"Okay, that's enough," says Coach. "Lucy, you need to go home. I think you need to rest and reflect on this. We can talk later."

"What? No! You can't be serious."

"Yes, I am. Look, Emily is captain because that's what the team needs right now. You need to take care of yourself and then come back ready to work."

"I'm ready now! I'm here. Do you have any idea how hard I've worked to get back here?"

"Yes, I do. Frankly, I'm concerned about you. So until you can show me that you can treat me and your teammates with respect, you're off the team."

"Off the team?" The words come out strangled.

Coach looks at me, her expression a mixture of disappointment and pity that cuts me to the core.

"But..." I can't speak, I'm so angry. But I don't want to cry in front of them.

Coach steers me away from the group. "Maybe your leg is healed," she says, more gently now. "But I need a fly-half who can keep her cool. How can I keep you and your teammates safe if you can't control your emotions?"

"I can't believe you're doing this to me." I feel the tears coming, and I'm powerless to stop them.

Coach sighs. "Lucy, I didn't want this conversation to go this way. Please, just listen to me when I tell you that your legs don't make you a great rugby player. Your mind is what's valuable. And until you have a healthy mindset, I can't let you back on the field."

I back away from her, grab my backpack and my water bottle and start to run.

Chapter Seventeen
The Hits Keep On Coming

My name is Lucy Graves and I don't know what I will do without rugby. As I storm off the field, Andy runs after me and has to call my name several times. I don't answer him until he grabs me by the shoulder.

I whirl around, tears streaming down my face. I do not want him to see me like this.

"Whoa," he says. "What happened back there?"

"Only my entire future going up in smoke," I say. I feel like I'm choking on the words. "Why did Emily tell me to ask you about the video? You know what I'm talking about, don't you?"

He sighs. "I am the one who shot the video."

"What? No."

"Yes," he says, "But I didn't edit it or add that horrible music or upload it to YouTube. It was my brother. He took my phone when I showed the footage to him, and afterward I couldn't get him to take it down. I'm so sorry."

"Sorry? You think that's going to cut it for making me the joke of the entire school?"

"Come on," he says. "It's not that big a deal."

"Not that big a deal? Have you met me? Do you even know what rugby means to me? What it meant to my father?"

"Your father?" he asks. "I don't understand. What does your dad have to do with anything?"

"Forget it. You wouldn't understand. I can't believe I ever trusted you."

"No, I don't understand," he says, his eyes flashing with anger. "Because you don't tell me what you're feeling. You just cover it all up with your weird obsessions and superstitions and silly...thingamabobs."

He grabs my backpack and takes out my trusty rugby ball.

"Like this ratty ball. What's the deal? You're seventeen, but you drag this thing around like a security blanket." He shakes his head.

"Give me back my father's ball," I say in a deadly quiet voice.

"Your...your father's..." He trails off and stares at me before gently handing it back.

I snatch it from him and hold it close.

"How would you know how I feel? You have the most average life ever. Nothing happens to you. Everything you do works out just fine. Your biggest problem is a bully of a big brother." My voice is getting louder, and I feel myself unraveling.

"You're right," he says, flatly. "I'm so lucky. My life is so perfect. I guess I have to be tortured like you are to be worthy, huh?"

"Tortured?" I chuckle sadly. "Try broken."

"Lucy," he starts, reaching for me.

"My dad died trying to save me," I say. I haven't said these words out loud in years, and I can't stop myself despite the horrified look on Andy's face. I know he will never see me the same way again.

"Oh my god," he says.

"Yeah. Oh my god." I shake my head, memories floating again to the surface. "I was 12. He was taking me to see a rugby sevens game, one of our little rituals. It was snowing. A guy flipped his pickup on the freeway, and our little jeep rolled a bunch of times and caught on fire. My dad had two broken legs, but he still got me out of there."

"I'm sorry," Andy says quietly. "I didn't know. I didn't mean it."

"Well, now you know," I say. "Go away, Andy. I don't want to see you anymore."

"Lucy, please." He steps toward me, but I back away.

"It's over," I say.

I turn and walk away. I don't look back.

Chapter Eighteen
Breaking Point

My name is Lucy Graves and my whole world is falling apart. When I get home, I'm exhausted. It's normally a forty-five-minute walk, but my ankle kept seizing up. As I enter the house I see Mom sitting on the couch. She's holding my notebook—the one I write my numbers and lists in when the outside world gets to be too much. I started doing it when I was 12.

I sigh. I already know everything she's going to say, so I just hold my hands u and sit down next to her.

"Lucy," she says. "I'm worried. What is this?" She motions to the book. "I thought you were past this."

I can only shrug.

"Is it starting again? You're already having panic attacks. I overlooked it because you've just been injured and I thought you'd move past it. But seeing this...I think you need help." Mom takes a breath.

I open my mouth to protest, but the look on her face tells me to keep quiet.

"I already spoke to Coach Stevens. When I called her she told me what happened today. She said how sorry she was that things worked out the way they did. I understand why she removed you from the team, and I think it was the right decision. She should not have pushed you so hard today, and I made clear to her all the sacrifices you have made for this team. She does not want to ban you from the team permanently, but I think maybe you need to take some time to decide whether this is something you want in your life."

"But...it's rugby."

She takes my hands in hers. "Lucy, honey, I am here for you. I love you all the time—you know that. I will do whatever it takes to support you. And I have booked an appointment with Dr. Chris."

"Mom, that's not necessary."

She shushes me. "It's just a follow-up. She can see you later tomorrow, and we'll go from there."

I spend the rest of the evening in my room, staring at the wall. Where did I go wrong? A few weeks ago I was Lucy Graves, rugby player. Now who am I?

I grab my rugby ball and head out the back door. Our house backs onto a little greenbelt, and I like to go back here to toss my ball and run after it. I walk to the edge of the grass, where it meets the bushes and trees. I look at my dad's old ball. I hold it out with my hands and then kick it as hard as I can. It sails through the air and lands deep in the trees.

I stare after it for a while and then lim? back home in the darkness. When I s back, Mom is waiting for me in the kitchen The dark circles under her eyes seem so much deeper. We look at each other in silence for a long time.

"Just say it, Lucy," she says. "You've been needing to say it for a long time."

"It was my fault he died." It comes out in a whisper.

"No, honey. No, it wasn't." She opens her arms as if to hug me.

I hold up my hands. "Yes, it was. Dad used to be lucky, and I took all of his luck just by being born. I used it up and then he died."

We're both crying, standing in the kitchen next to the dirty dishes.

"Baby, it doesn't work like that," Mom says.

"How do you know?" I have a terrible thought. "Oh, Mom, what if I'm using up all your luck too? What if...?" I can barely say it out loud.

"Lucy," Mom says, grabbing me and pulling me close. "I'm here. Right now. And everything is okay."

"If it weren't for me, he'd still be alive," I whimper into her shoulder.

She brushes my hair back from my forehead. "Your dad would hate to see you like this. He loved you, and he loved his life. Even at the end he died doing what was most important to him. Keeping you safe."

She pauses, letting this sink in. "I know you're struggling. I also know that you are your father's daughter. You're not going to let an injury keep you from achieving your dreams."

I nod, too shredded to speak.

"So what do you want?" Mom asks. "Do you want to quit rugby for good and let it all go? You can do that."

"No, I want to keep playing," I say, my voice a whisper.

"Then let's get to work, because it's going to be hard."

"Mom," I say. "Can you help me with something first?"

"Anything."

Minutes later we're armed with flashlights and searching the woods for my b

We're about to give up when I see a glint of reflective tape dangling from a branch overhead. Nestled in a tree, in a branch just low enough to reach, is my dad's ball.

"Well, look at that," says Mom. "How many points?"

"I don't know—that's at least a three-pointer." I grab the ball out of the tree and Mom leads the way back home, her flashlight darting in the night.

I tuck the ball back under my arm, bring it into my room and place it up on my shelf. It's going to have to stay here from now on. I'll keep it, but I won't let it control me anymore.

Chapter Nineteen
Treatment

My name is Lucy Graves and I am in therapy. Again. My therapist is a cool lady named Dr. Chris. She helped me a lot after Dad died, and I'm relieved when I see her today. She thinks I'm going to be fine. Breaking my ankle triggered the post-traumatic stress disorder I've struggled with ever since the car accident that killed my dad. It didn't help that my OCD decided to spiral out of control too, but Dr. Chris is encouraged by the support I have from Mom and by my new perspective.

"You know, Lucy, anxiety is common in athletes. You've chosen a high-pressure path in life. You'll need to make some hard decisions and work on your coping skills if you want to build a career." Dr. Chris doesn't waste time getting to the point.

"I know," I say. "I'm ready to work on it. No more rituals, no more superstition. I've got to ask people for help."

"Yes, you do," says Dr. Chris. "It sounds like you have a lot of people who care about you. Let them be there for you. There is a difference between the healthy structure of routine and the obsession of rituals. It can be tricky to find the balance. So instead, why not focus on the truly important question: how can you rediscover your love of the game?"

"Yeah, I don't know when I stopped loving the game for the game's sake. I used to love everything about rugby, right back to when my dad first taught me about passing the ball backward instead forward. I remember thinking that was at."

Dr. Chris nods. "Your anxiety stems from trying to live either in the past or in the future. But try to remember that the only time that exists is now. How about trying to play rugby in the now?"

Play in the now. Sounds good to me.

Dr. Chris advises me to put away my number filled notebooks for a while. It is hard at first, but with therapy and practice, I'm told, it will get easier. I take a few days to rest at home before going back to school.

As soon as I'm back, I find Coach Stevens in her gym office between periods. I'm expecting her to be annoyed with me, but instead she greets me with a warm smile.

"Lucy, good to see you. Come on in."

"Hi," I say, feeling shy. "Um, Coach. I'm sorry for the way I acted. I wasn't...I was having a hard time."

Coach shakes her head. "I'm sorry too. You've been through so much, and I put too much pressure on you. When your mom called, she was pretty livid with

I suppose I didn't realize what all of this has been like for you. I'm used to my players being tough and playing through injuries and training hard, but you're seventeen. And you should be having fun."

"Okay," I say. "Thanks."

"You have a good mom. And I'd like you to come back if you think it's something you want."

"Back on the team? Hell yes," I say.

Coach laughs. "That's the Lucy Graves I know. Now get to class before your mom calls me again."

On the way to math class I run into Emily in the hall. We approach each other cautiously. I'm not sure I'm ready for this, but I know I've got to make things right.

"Hey," says Emily, breaking the awkward silence. "I heard you're doing better."

I nod. "Yeah. I am. Look, Emily, I was really mad at you, but the truth is, you deserve to be captain. I just couldn't handle it. I was jealous. I don't know what else to say."

She smiles. "Well," she says. "I guess you know what it feels like."

"What do you mean?"

"Come on, Lucy. You're perfect. It's disgusting."

"Me? Emily Jones, I defy you to name one thing that's not perfect about you."

She hesitates, suppressing a laugh. "Promise not to tell anyone?"

I shrug. "Yeah."

"I like to watch pimple-popping videos online."

"What? No. That's disgusting."

"Yes, the grosser the better."

We both break into hysterical laughter, and passing students give us weird looks. It feels good to let all the tension go.

"God, I needed that," I say, wiping away a tear.

"You know what else you need?" Emily asks.

I raise an eyebrow at her, and she giggles.

"It's enchilada day," she says.

"No way."

"Oh yes. And if we hurry we can b the rush. You in?"

"Always, Em."

We hurry off down the hall, half running, raving about the salty chicken enchiladas our cafeteria is famous for. It's as if nothing happened. I'm so lucky to have a friend like Emily.

Chapter Twenty
One Plus One

After Emily and I stuff ourselves with record-breaking amounts of enchiladas (and a serving of nachos with liquid cheese as a chaser), I waddle off to AP Math lab. I feel sick because I'm full of high-sodium cafeteria food, but also because Andy will be there. He must hate me.

When I get to the lab I take a breath and walk in. Andy isn't here.

I approach Mr. McCabe. "Um, hi," I s? "I'm sorry I haven't been in class."

He smiles at me. "It's okay. I understand. And you know, if there's anything you ever need or anything you want to talk about, my door is always open."

"Thanks," I say. "Actually, there is one thing."

"Name it."

"Well, I've always wanted to know what's up with your wall plaques."

"Ah, my signs. Yes." He leans back in his chair and takes a breath. "Cheesy, huh? My mother liked them. But she's been gone for a while now. When I look at them I don't see wood and paint. I see her."

"Oh," I say, feeling like a fool. "I'm so sorry. I had no idea."

"It's okay, Lucy. I'm a teacher. You're not supposed to see me as a real person."

He smiles at me, giving me a goofy look, and I laugh.

"Thanks," I say.

"Don't mention it. You could thank me ꞋΧ joining Mathletes."

"Sorry, Mr. McCabe. I'm trying to take a ꞋΧack from activities right now."

He nods. "That's probably wise, Lucy." He clears his throat and nods toward the door, indicating for me to look.

I turn and see that Andy is leaning against the doorframe in an awkward-but-trying-to-be-nonchalant pose. He's holding a new rugby ball wrapped in red ribbon, and he shifts it from hand to hand as if he doesn't quite know how to hold it.

"Save me, Lucy Graves. I have no idea what I'm doing," he says.

"That's okay," I say. "I don't either." I walk over to him and throw my arms around him, knocking the ball to the floor. I don't care who sees.

"Whoa," he says. "That was easier than I thought."

I laugh. "I guess it's just your lucky day."

Chapter Twenty-One
Second Chances

My name is Lucy Graves and I am going to be okay. Coach is helping me get over my fear by running a tackle-only practice today. I'm going to run down the length of the pitch at full speed, and every single player is going to take a turn bringing me down.

"You ready for this?" Coach asks. "Our big game is against the Grizzlies. They won ll their semis, so it's us against them. I'd ally understand if you want to sit this ut."

"It's a beautiful day," I reply, choosing to brush it off as I make my way onto the field. The air is brisk and clean, and the grass is firm and dry. I feel my rugby boots dig in as I jog to one end of the pitch and take my position on the try line. I toe the white paint and look down at my right ankle. My calf is still a centimeter smaller in circumference than my left because I haven't yet gained back all the muscle I lost. But otherwise my leg is as strong as it's ever been.

I take a deep breath and stretch my arms overhead, looking to the sky, at that bright blue expanse, and then swoop forward and touch the earth between my feet, feeling the stretch down my hamstrings and calves. I come back up and rotate my hips, knees and ankles, spending extra time flexing my right and making sure it's warm and filled with blood.

All along the sidelines my team lines up—twenty-one girls in blue jerseys. Some are tall, some are short. Some are wiry and some are stocky. Most have bruises up and down their legs. And a few have stitch

A cut lip, a bruised brow, a knee brace, a bad scrape. We're all roughed up because we're all rough. We're rugby players. As I look at them lined up and waiting to throw their bodies at me, to try their best to bring me down for my sake and for theirs, I remember what it is I love so much about this game. When we're out on the field it's a battle, and we have to be there for each other—to find the space or close the gaps—and we're willing to take the hits and the pain for one another. We're a team, and we win or lose together.

Coach blows her whistle and I take off, pumping hard with my knees as I drive down the field. If they want to tackle me, I'm not going to make it easy.

I race past the first tackler, Samantha. As I hurtle past, widely escaping her reach, I hear her call out, "Go, Lucky!"

Next is Jenny, who tries to get the better of me by running at me straight on, but I quickly spin and sidestep her.

"Go, Lucy!" yells Coach.

That's all the encouragement I need. I pick up even more speed, and I swear I'm feeling faster than I've ever been. Maybe all the extra training and good nutrition has made my game stronger than before. Maybe breaking my ankle really was lucky.

I run hard, keeping the try line in my sights. I know the next tackle is Emily. This will be tough because Emily is fast, and I know she's not going to let me get away with anything. She zips past me but doubles around and is now fully chasing me down the field. The other girls are hooting and yelling, encouraging us both. They alternately yell for me to make it and for Emily to take me down. I'm having the time of my life.

When I feel her tackle me I'm not scared. Emily's arms circling my waist, her weight pulling me to the ground. We tumble, knees and elbows knocking together, heads bonking, cleats scraping each other's legs, and we come to a rest o the turf. Instinctively I let go of the b but the moment is brief, for as soon as Emily releases me, I'm up again. I grab the ball and start running. She might have taken me down, but not for long!

I zip toward that try line, and no one else is quick enough to nab me. I run across, and just to prove to myself that I'm not afraid to fall, I dive to touch the ball down in the in-goal zone, rolling over and over on myself until I come to a rest beneath the posts. I'm alive. I'm unhurt. I can play rugby again.

I take a moment to drink it in, staring up at the bright sky, feeling truly lucky and alive. Coach blows her whistle. It's time to get my butt up to do it all again.

We spend the rest of the afternoon this way, with the others mercilessly tackling me, so often that any residual fear vanishes. I love the hits. I love the pain. I love rugby.

When practice is over, the girls offer to ke me for ice cream. The old Lucy would e begged off, but I accept. Before we Coach calls us over.

"Ladies," she says to all of us. "In light of your recent impressive accomplishment in sport, the tightwads in this district have given us a little extra money to celebrate the Eagles having made it so far in the season. We've got a little money for a post-season banquet. And we have also had those ancient jerseys of yours updated. They're still blue, but now the eagle graphic actually looks like an eagle. So, congratulations! Next year, maybe they'll see about fixing this field up for us too. All right, come and get them."

Coach opens up a box, and we all come forward to get our jerseys. She reaches in and pulls out my number 10. I see that it has the C stitched on the shoulder.

"Um, Coach," I say. "I think this is a mistake."

"What are you saying, Lucy?"

"I'm saying that Emily stepped up while I was down, and she showed herself to be a good captain. I think she should keep the position."

Emily looks at me, her eyes wide.

Coach nods. "Well, I considered that, Lucy, and I'm glad you feel that way."

"Good," I say. "So it's settled."

"Nope," says Coach, reaching into the box. She pulls out Emily's number 8 and tosses it to her. It also has a C on it.

"What? No..." says Emily, but she is smiling wide. She looks at me. "So we're—"

"Co-captains!" says Coach. "I don't know why I didn't think of it before. You guys make a great team. Emily, you're—"

"Fast, solid, reliable, smart," I say, and Emily grins at me.

Coach laughs. "And Lucy, you're—"

"Brave," says Emily.

I don't know what to say, so I just hold out my hands. All my girls come in for our team's version of a hug, which is kind of like a violent smash.

"Let's go get that ice cream," I say, and we all scramble off the field, excited for the game ahead, our new jerseys and the promise of a united team.

Chapter Twenty-Two
Learning To Play

My name is Lucy Graves and I am playing rugby again. "Stay in the moment, Lucy. The only thing that exists is right here, right now." I keep telling myself this as I shake my legs out and warm up on the field with my team.

The Grizzlies have arrived, and the stands are filling up with spectators. I see Formerly Evil Number 12 arrive too. She seemed pretty shaken up at the time by what happened, and as she arrives she gives me a little nod. She's not entirely forgiven but I know she's just trying to win like th rest of us. I can't hate her for that. But I'm still going to beat her.

The good news is we're playing on the Grizzlies' brand-new turf. There's not a pothole to be found, which is great because the rain is already coming down in sheets. There are huge floodlights and an actual electronic scoreboard. I look up at it and know that I've got to do everything to get the score going in our favor. The downside of being on this nice new field is the Grizzlies have home advantage, and the crowd is full of their supporters.

I look to my left, at our section of the bleachers, and see Mom waving at me. She has a T-shirt with the name Graves printed on it.

There's Andy, looking nervous and adorable, holding a sign that says *I HEART #10*.

Mr. McCabe is here too, along with several Blue Mountain High students who made the trek to cheer us on.

I take all of them in, remembering what Dr. Chris said about trusting the people around me.

I look over at Emily. "I just want you to know that we're going to crush them."

She breaks into a huge grin. "Hell yeah, we are."

I wave to Coach. She's been watching me, no doubt worrying, but when I give her the thumbs-up, I see her shoulders relax a little.

The ref blows his whistle. The game is about to start.

My name is Lucy Graves and this is a grudge match. It's a hard game, filled with questionable calls, and many of the tackles are borderline illegal. But it's a championship match. Play can't be stopped for every little infraction.

It's deep into the second half. After back-and-forth gains both teams are badly roughed up. We're covered in scrapes and bruises and fighting for every point in the pouring rain.

We're losing 15–10 when Jenny gets a breakaway. I watch as she leaps acro the field and takes a hard hit from a huge Grizzly prop. I run over to her. Her left eyebrow is split open and bleeding. I help her to the sideline, where Coach presses gauze to the wound to try to stop the bleeding.

"Coach," says Jenny, "don't sub me. I'm fine."

If a player subs out because of a "blood injury," she can only return as long as she's not out longer than ten minutes.

I look at Coach. "How fast can she get stitched?"

"Not fast enough."

Our alternate, Wendy Jensen, runs onto the field, looking equal parts terrified and excited. Emily grabs her and starts strategizing as we all run over for the scrum.

We need to get possession. The clock will run out soon, and we need to score to tie up this game. As the scrum forms I watch closely, hoping our hooker will snag the ball and get it to Emily. She does, and I see our one opportunity to tie things up.

One of the strategies we've been working our "run at 'em" tactic. Any time we're trying to overcome a loss of speed, or we're afraid the other team is going to take us down hard, the plan is to run straight at them. It sounds crazy and counterintuitive, but when you run directly at an opponent you take away their advantage. It's the same as facing a fear head-on. The key is that when you run directly at an opponent, you fix them in position. They're the ones who get stuck. Not you.

I've been waiting for the right time, when I'm near the Grizzlies' in-goal area and able to surprise them. All I need is for Emily to feed me a killer pass on the fly, and I'll be able to exploit the weakness in their defensive line.

Emily snaps me the ball, and I move into the socket of space twenty meters from their try line. I start to run and look up to see Formerly Evil Number 12 bearing down on me from the blindside. I'm not going to let her take me out sideways again. It takes every ounce of guts I have, but I just grit my teeth and run straight at her. I know I'm going to win, because I jus changed this game from a race to an agility contest. Formerly Evil Number 12 is fast, but she's huge, and I know I can evade her. I need her to get close to me.

We run full speed at each other. I hear Coach yelling and the crowd going nuts, and I'm sure they think I'm insane, but I have no intention of trying to crash through her.

She is close now. It's do-or-die time.

Chapter Twenty-Three
Redemption

My name is Lucy Graves and I'm yards from oblivion. Formerly Evil Number 12 is bearing down on me, and she lowers her head as she draws near. When she's close enough to me to reach out and grab me, I leap to the right in midstride, spinning in the air, and do a quick rugby jig around her. She blows past me with all her momentum and force.

I point myself toward her try line, just nine meters out now, and run for my life. I know she'll be coming for me, but I'm hoping the sidestep bought me a couple seconds' leeway. The clock is ticking down, and I need to get there. I hear the crowd screaming out the time. "Six, five, four, three..."

On the count of "two," I touch down over the try line, falling with the ball in my hands to score the most important points I've ever scored.

"One."

The buzzer for full time sounds, and the crowd alternately yells and groans, but there are enough Eagles fans in the stands that it's a celebratory ruckus. We haven't lost, but we haven't won. It's a 20–20 tie.

There are no shootouts or tiebreakers in rugby, and we won't be content with a draw. We need to beat the Grizzlies, and we know they'll be doing everything they can to beat us too.

After a five-minute break we now, as the rules dictate, move into extra time, playing two ten-minute halves in full. At the end of that extra time, whoever has scored the most points wins. We try our best for a grudging twenty minutes, coming close to scoring several times, but each time we are shut down by the Grizzlies' defense. We don't let them score either, and by the end of extra time all we have to show for it are two teams of exhausted girls. It feels like this game will never end. I try to remind myself to enjoy the moment. I'm playing rugby!

So now we have to head into sudden death. We will play another ten minutes of regular rugby, but this time the first team to score any points at all wins. The risky nature of sudden death gets us all amped up again. We have a quick huddle and agree that our best shot is for me to try to kick the ball deep into the Grizzly zone while Emily makes a break for it. The key is gaining possession first, and that's where the rest of the team comes in. The Grizzlies win the toss and chip-kick the ball into our end, but Sabrina snatches it up in a blistering cross-pitch run, hurtles past me and chucks it back. I'm already on the ball, plucking it from the air and running hard, with Emily right behind me.

"Now!" I shout, kicking the ball hard and high.

Emily shoots past me, running faster than I have ever seen her go. She has to get to the ball before it hits the ground and before any Grizzlies catch it.

She catches the ball midstride, and she's so close to the end. I'm running after her, my lungs screaming. We're almost there. A big Grizzly defender comes in for a tackle, but Emily sidesteps her with ease.

She's a few meters from scoring when the buzzer sounds. We are out of time.

Emily runs through to the try line anyway and then turns back, defeated.

I jog up to her. "That was the closest we were ever going to come," I say. "Time just wasn't on our side. You were amazing. So fast."

She nods, but I can tell she's upset.

The only thing left now is the kicking competition. I don't know whether to be elated or anxious about this. We clearly have the advantage because our team has several strong kickers to choose from, but the pressure is so heavy you can practically chew it.

Each team must nominate one player to kick, and our team immediately chooses me.

I hesitate. "You know, Emily is a strong kicker too."

"But you've got this," says Emily. "I don't have the talent you have for angles, and you know how tough this competition is. Our best chance is with you."

"I agree," says Coach. "I wish it didn't come down to this, Lucy, but I want you to know that whatever happens with the kicks, we played good rugby today. We can be proud of this game."

I look across the field at the Grizzlies, at how tired and nervous they look. They want it just as bad. I hope they all have friends as good as mine.

"Okay," I say. "Let's finish this. I can do it."

The Grizzlies nominate their own fly-half to take the kicks. She steps up and we look at each other, each of us a mirror reflection. We're two tired athletes covered in mud and scraped up. All each of us wants is to win for our team, and we're both no doubt feeling the pressure. We each have to attempt two place kicks from set positions on three different areas of the field, all on the twenty-two-meter line. The first area is dead center in front of the posts. The second is to the left of the posts fifteen meters in from the touch line. The third is to the right of the posts fifteen meters in from the touch line. At the world-cup level there would be a couple more kicking positions closer to the try line, but in our league we keep it a bit simpler.

We will each take our kicks, and after we are both done, the team of whoever scores more goals wins the match. If we're still tied, we must repeat the procedure until someone wins. The first kick is supposed to be taken by the team that had possession of the ball at the very start of the match. Since the Grizzlies chose possession after winning the coin toss, that means the Grizzlies go first. I'm secretly happy about this. It gives me a moment to breathe and calm myself down.

I watch as their fly-half takes her first position. She is allowed up to one minute to complete the kick. She takes her shot and scores. The crowd cheers.

I try not to let it rattle me. The center position is easiest. I've done this hundreds of times in practice, and I can do it now. This is where all my hard work will pay off.

The ref motions for me to come forward, and I take my position. He gives me the go-ahead, and I take a moment to still myself. *Breathe, Lucy. Just breathe.* I ground myself in my body, feeling my legs planted firmly. I feel strong. I kick the ball, and it's a clean shot that sails through my target. Score. My team cheers, and I'm relieved to get one on the board.

The next two kicks we each take are from the left positions. The Grizzly fly-half and I both nail our marks. Still tied.

Finally we get set to take two kicks each from the right position. As the Grizzly fly-half takes her first shot, I see her waver a bit, and the ball doesn't quite get the air it needs. No score.

She tries again and scores on her final shot. Now it's down to me. I need to score one goal to keep the game tied, and two goals to win.

I line up my first shot and take the kick, and it sails perfectly over the posts. Score!

We're tied again. I let out the breath I've been holding. Just one more.

"Come on, Lucy!" I hear my mom calling from the stands. I turn and look, and she's on her feet with Andy. They look so excited and proud that I know I'll be okay whatever happens. Maybe I'll make this shot and maybe I won't, but I've got everything a girl could ever want.

The ref points at me, letting me know it's time for me to kick. I focus on the oval ball. Nothing exists right now except for my body, my legs, my feet and this ball. I take a breath and hold it, bringing my leg back and then forward in a graceful arc, hitting the ball with my right instep, letting out my breath at the same time.

I feel a good connection on the strike, my leg swinging from the hip, and I watch the ball with my eyes. It sails upward into the now blue sky.

The angle is tight, but it looks like it's going to make it. Just a few centimeters one way and we will win. A hush falls over the field as we all fly with the ball, willing it to clear. I'm praying I don't hear the sound of it clanging against the post.

The ref holds up his arms. It's good. I scored. *We won.*

I fall to my knees on the pitch and am surrounded by my team. They pick me up and crush into me with their one-of-a-kind Eagles scrum-hug. There is no better feeling in the world.

Who am I?

I sit at my desk, finally ready to write the scholarship essay I've been putting off. The deadline is in two days, so I don't have much choice, but it's not hard to answer this question anymore. I've got to hurry up, though, because Andy is taking me to the rugby banquet tonight. He said he even bought me a corsage, which is the dorkiest, most adorable thing he's done so far. I told him it would look fabulous with my rugby jersey. The other girls are never going to let me live this one down.

I look at the rugby ball he bought me. It's sitting on the shelf, right next to my dad's. I take down the old ball and place it on my desk in front of me. It's time to finally write about this. Even though it felt like the world was ending when I broke my ankle—just like it felt when Dad died—I've realized that I can get through anything. I just need to count on the people in my life. Mom, Andy, Emily, my team. As I write my final list, I know that Dad would be so proud of me. It feels like winning all over again.

I AM:

1. A championship-winning rugby player and the best fly-half Blue Mountain High has ever seen.

2. A trauma survivor, a viral video and a comeback story.
3. A teammate, a friend, a girlfriend and a daughter.

I am the luckiest girl alive.

Acknowledgments

Once upon a time I played rugby, loved it and then injured myself. Since then I've taken up a permanent seat on the sidelines, so I'd like to thank this rough and intelligent sport for inspiring my book. Hard work beats luck any day, it's true, but it's also true that I am very fortunate. I get to live my dream, writing young adult fiction, and I get to work with all the awesome folks at Orca Book Publishers. Thank you for bringing this little book to life. And thank you, always, to my family.

Author's Note

A novel about girls playing rugby simply must have an amazing player on its cover, and I am honored that an image of the incredible Chanelle Edwards-Challenger graces this book. Chanelle, a center for the University of Victoria women's rugby team (GO, VIKES, GO!), is a Canada West Champion, an all-star and an All-Canadian, which means she did all this *and* got good grades too. She embodies everything Lucy "Lucky" Graves hopes to be.

Rugby is a girl sport. It's tough, it's fast, and it can take you places. The players on the women's national rugby team come from every corner of Canada. And the team consistently places in the top five in the world.

I like to imagine that shortly after this action shot was taken, Chanelle evaded the tackle and scored the winning try. But even if she didn't, I'm sure she got right back into the game. Because that's what winners do.

For information about the UVic Vikes Rugby Academy for girls aged fourteen to seventeen, visit govikesgo.com.

Brooke Carter is the author of the Orca Soundings titles *Another Miserable Love Song* and *Learning Seventeen*. She was born and raised in beautiful British Columbia, where she earned an MFA in Creative Writing (UBC) and where she currently lives with her family. For more information, visit brookecarter.com.

orca sports

For more information on all the books
in the Orca Sports series, please visit
orcabook.com